About the author

April Coughlan Wong has a Bachelor of Arts Degree in English from the University of Alberta and a Graduate Certificate in Journalism from the University of Queensland. With over fifteen years' writing and reporting experience in television and advertising, April is thrilled to be applying her passion for the written word to her first love of fiction. April lives in Calgary, Canada, with her husband, two daughters and golden retriever.

DEATH & DAHLIA

April Coughlan Wong

DEATH & DAHLIA

Vanguard Press

A CIP catalogue record for this title is
available from the British Library.

ISBN 978 1 784659 90 5

*Vanguard Press is an imprint of
Pegasus Elliot MacKenzie Publishers Ltd.*
www.pegasuspublishers.com

First Published in 2021

**Vanguard Press
Sheraton House Castle Park
Cambridge England**

Printed & Bound in Great Britain

Dedication

Dearest Everly and Gwendolyn, you will always have a friend in me.

And to the memory of my Grandma Betty, whose love of books was outmatched only by the love she held for her family.

Acknowledgements

I would like to thank the following:

First and foremost, to my husband, Joey. I am constantly in awe of your selflessness and dedication to our family. I know how incredibly blessed I am to go through this life with you by my side. Your unwavering support and enthusiasm on every single one of my crazy whims and pursuits means more to me than anything. Thank you for giving me the space and time to do the things that make me, *me*, so that I am present for you and the girls as the best version of myself. Somehow you figured that out long before I did, and I am forever grateful. (Sorry about not including that nurse character.)

To Laura and Natasha, your encouragement for me to take this leap of faith began on an ominous winding road in Montana and continued throughout this entire process. Thank you for believing in me more than I did.

To Kristen, for the hours of chats and texts and giving me the best compliment of my life. I'm hoping you'll make an exception and add this to your reading list.

To the Bunco Ladies. I'm fortunate to be part of a group of women who build each other up and cheer each other on. You have helped me to be a better mom and a better friend. And don't think I've forgotten the promise of a big book party.

To my family, from the ones I was born into to the ones I've picked up along the way, thank you for all your love and support. This especially includes Branden and Christine. Thank you for Papa Mondays that gave me much-needed time for this writing process.

To Grandpa and Grandma German, whose infamous farm was the inspiration for this story; but also, it is thanks to their generosity that this book happened at all.

To Dad: you have always believed in me no matter what I set out to achieve (except maybe playing softball or a career as a mathematician).

To my sister Laura, who passionately cheers me on in everything I do, big or small. Thank you for being my therapist, comic relief, partner in crime, sounding board, best friend and proof reader.

To Mom, thank you for reading my first draft and encouraging me to keep going. I will forever treasure that message you sent. One of the hardest parts of this process was the absolute imagination it took to write mothers who were anything short of perfect, because that has been my only experience. I strive every day to be the kind of mom I had, for my children.

And last but, of course, never least, to my precious daughters, Everly and Gwendolyn. "Life will never be the same," and I wouldn't want it to be. It is the greatest honour of my life to be your mom. Everly, when I heard you bragged to a kindergarten friend that your mom is a "writer, like a real writer", I knew all this effort was worth it. There is nothing more meaningful than to have your child be proud of you. Thanks to you girls, I have nothing to prove, because to the ones that matter most, I'm already somebody.

Chapter One
Dahlia — DD in 54 years, 9 months, 13 days

I wake up confused and disoriented. How long had I been asleep? My back is soaked and I'm shivering from the cold sweat that has pooled underneath me. My eyes are swollen and crusted shut from crying. As I rub away the sleep from the corners, I open them enough to see the dull light coming into the room from the window. It must be late afternoon. I still feel exhausted and pull up the blanket to cover myself and try to slip back to sleep. I reach down to wrap my arms around my stomach to feel the warmth and bulge of my belly as I've done for months, but it feels different. What was once a hard-tight ball, now feels soft and doughy. In a split second, everything that happened in the last day snaps back into focus and I bolt straight up with fear. I can see a bassinet beside me.

She's here.
She's safe.
She's perfect.
And he's gone.

***

Twenty-four hours before

"Everything is going to be fine. Your daughter has lost a lot of blood. Your partner has listed his blood type as O negative, so he can donate his blood to her for the transfusion and she's going to be okay. You just rest now."

I'm still trying to process all of this information in my medicated, exhausted haze. I was so worried about the baby, but I could barely keep my eyes open. As they wheeled her bassinet out of the hospital room, I saw him follow behind, looking concerned but elated all at the same time. I knew as long as he was with her, she would be okay. He was our great protector and would do everything he could to take care of us.

I must have drifted off to sleep, when I am gently nudged awake by a nurse. She said it was time to try feeding again and that the baby had received her blood transfusion from her father and she was already getting stronger. "She just needs to nurse and have some skin-to-skin time with her mom." This was the kind-eyed nurse who had deep smile lines and a very soft sing-songy voice that in any other circumstance would have irritated me; but in this setting, it was reassuring. Nursing and skin-to-skin were terms that sounded vaguely familiar. If it wasn't for him reading aloud chapters of *What to Expect When You're Expecting* while I worked away on my computer for all those months, I would have no idea what the nurse was talking about.

"Here, let me help you." I was grateful for her assistance, and together we got the baby fed and nestled in, naked against my bare chest. I was starting to feel like I would doze off again and asked the nurse if she knew where my boyfriend was.

"He left right after the transfusion. I saw him heading out of the maternity ward. We asked him to sit down for a while, that he might be light-headed after giving blood, but he said he was fine. I assumed you knew where he was headed." I must have had a confused look on my face, as the nurse was checking over all the machines I was hooked up to.

"You two are a very special couple. I can't imagine how hard this pregnancy and birth must have been for you, knowing he's only got six months left to live." She looked down at my sleeping baby and shook her head. "At least he'll have some time to get to know this little angel."

"Sorry, what did you say? Six months? What do you mean?"

"We scanned his ParColm Vial before taking his blood. I assumed you knew his life expectancy. He's a Vita Brevis. He has six months four days and thirteen hours until he dies."

Chapter Two
Milo — DD in 0 years, 6 months, 4 days

I had to quietly slip past the night-shift nurse at the desk. I still have my hospital bracelet on, so I didn't have any issue getting back into the maternity ward. I just couldn't afford to draw attention to myself now. As I sit in the bulky leather chair at the end of the foot of her bed, I can see her eyes flutter and twitch while she dreams. She has never been a peaceful sleeper, always thrashing arms, legs and blankets around. But now she is still. Her body has been through so much and must have surrendered to sleeping motionless for once. Wide awake in my arms is the baby girl I was so desperate to meet. I didn't know if I'd get a chance to hold her, so I am memorising every detail, from her tiny button nose, her sharp little fingernails to the uneven pattern of blonde hair swirling around the top of her head. I think she looks a little like me. It's her eyes. Maybe I'll live on through them.

I know I can't stay the night. There are going to be too many questions that I don't have answers for. Or at least not the answers that would keep me alive. I reach for the blanket I'd packed in the hospital bag and swaddle her up in the way I'd practised at home over and over on a pillow. I had read all the books and done all the research. Dahlia hadn't been so sure about this parenting thing, but I had been sure enough for the both of us.

Once she is all wrapped back up, I lay her down in the bassinet beside her mom. I reach into the hospital bag and pull out the one thing that I'd wanted to share with my child from my childhood. As I read from the pages of a book I know by heart, I'm devastated thinking about all the nights I was expecting to read this to her. Those are now gone. I leave the book tucked in beside her and kiss Dahlia on the forehead. I leave the room as quietly as I entered it, without looking back at the life I so desperately dreamed of and can no longer be a part of.

Chapter Three
Dahlia — DD in 54 years, 9 months, 12 days

My first thought as I wake up is that I finally feel like I got some rest and the haziness from the medication has finally worn off. My body is feeling better, but I am aching in a different way. What a feeling to fall in love and have your heart broken in the same day. I sit myself up and look down into the bassinet and see my sweet baby still asleep peacefully beside me. A whistling noise comes from her nose with every breath. Although I am sore, I am longing to hold her close to me and fill the gap in my heart her dad has left. As I reach down to pick her up, I notice beside her is his little blue book. Tears sting my already sore, puffy eyes as I flip open the inside page and see there is a message. One hot tear drops onto the inscription, smearing the first few letters.

To my girls.
When you read this book, think of me and know that I am with you both always.
Trust in me. This is not the end, and I will make this right.

That was it. No more explanation than that. Just more questions. I turn to the first page and start to read.

On the night you were born, the moon smiled with such wonder that the stars peeked in to see you and the night wind whispered, "life will never be the same…"

I stop myself from reading any more. No kidding, life will never be the same. How could he do this? He was the one who wanted this family, while I was the one who took convincing. He was so excited to be a dad. How could he have lied to me about how much time he had left? We had talked about our life expectancies. We were both Vita Longas, over seventy-five years old, but now in my emotional, exhausted state I can't seem to remember what exact Death Date he had. We hadn't been dating that long before I found out I was pregnant, and as soon as that happened everything became about the baby and our commitment to each other, and spending our lives together was just assumed. So maybe I didn't know him as well as I thought I did. He certainly didn't seem like the kind of person who would want to have a baby with only six months to live! Why would he not tell me? And where has he gone?

Before I can wallow any more in my self-pity, the baby starts to cry out from her bassinet. I pick her up to feed her, but struggle to get her to latch on. Everything hurts, and whatever I am doing is just making the baby cry harder. I keep trying to adjust her and me, but have no luck. Her whole body becomes rigid from frustration and her sweet little face gets beet-red from crying. She starts screaming little rapid-fire-sounding cries and then I start crying, too. How is the most natural process in the world, where my body produces food for her to eat, also the most difficult and complicated? We struggle through our tears for what feels like forever, before the kind-eyed nurse come into the room.

"Oh, dear. Someone is not a happy camper," she says. "Let's try something else." She shows me a different way to hold the baby which seems completely counter-intuitive, but within a couple of seconds the baby latches on and begins feeding, and I let out a huge sigh of relief. "Don't get discouraged, dear. This doesn't usually happen easily for anyone. You are doing a great job."

***

As I start to pack up our room and get ready to leave the hospital, I have to swallow down the lumps in my throat. The little pink and white striped onesie 'going home' outfit was one he had chosen. Her blankets and soothers, everything packed up so neatly and methodically in the bag, was all him. He did all the research and read every review to make sure we'd got the safest car seat, and now I am struggling with the thick straps at the back, trying to tighten it up enough to secure this peaceful sleeping baby who is oblivious that she is left with the parent least likely to know what the hell they're doing. Or maybe not. I wouldn't have left her. So, I already win as the better parent. It seems like I've quickly moved from the denial phase of grief into the anger part. And with that thought, I realise I should call my mom. As the phone rings and rings, a cranky old nurse comes into the room carrying a folder of papers. With a sad and elitist expression on her face, she tells me they are our discharge papers. As I balance the phone between my chin and neck, holding up a finger to signal that I need a minute, that I'm obviously busy, she starts talking anyway. "How will you be getting home?" she says in a very judgemental tone. I doubt they deal with too many moms abandoned on the day of delivery. I asked if she could call me a cab, a sarcastic comment that falls flat on her.

"My sister is coming soon. Don't worry. But she has a motorcycle. Will that be a problem?" I don't know why I'm unleashing my pent-up fury on someone whose job it is to just ensure this brand-new innocent life has a safe ride home. I am completely exasperated, so someone has to take my lashings, and I'm determined not to let it be that sweet baby — so if not this nurse, then mom.

"H-helloo?" My mother finally answers the phone breathlessly and annoyed, as if whatever was on the other line couldn't possibly be as important as what she was doing.

I can just see her removing one dirty gardening glove with her teeth to hold the phone. A phone, still attached to a wall, with a cord, hanging in their shed. "That thing should be in a museum," I said the last time I was home. That was two years ago.

"Hi, Mom, it's Dahlia. I just want…"

"Dahlia, hello, sweetheart. Your father and I were just talking about you this morning. The daffodils are just poking through the ground and they are always up for your birthday; but with the weather we've had this winter, everything is so delayed."

"Daffodils — right. Well, it has been a really long, cold winter. But it should be finally warming up here now."

The weather. Always the weather. But when your parents own a greenhouse and that's how they have made a living for thirty years, the weather is pretty important.

"How's Dad?" I say quietly. I hold my breath and wait for her to exhale hers on the other end of the line. She might as well be on the other side of the country, not just a two-hour drive away.

"He's doing well. We both are. I mean, we've been busy with the auctions. Most of the farm equipment has sold and the realtor came by last week for us to sign the paperwork on the sale of the land. We got a better price than we could have hoped for the hundred acres. It's gone to a developer, so it will be hard to see the land turned into condos or something horrific; but we kept the plot overlooking the lake, and I'll still have the house and enough room to have a small market garden. One of the conditions on the sale was that they couldn't break ground until after September. That way, your Dad will be dead and won't have to see it."

That was Mom. She was blunt and accepting about death. Or she was locked in her greenhouse for days at a time.

"You'll be home for the Death, won't you, Dahlia?"

"Yes, of course, Mom. I'm going to be there when Dad dies. But I called… I called because… I had the baby yesterday. Early… the baby is born." The strangest sentence I'd ever formed came blurting out of my mouth. Dad will be dead. I had a baby. With death comes life, or some philosophical crap like that.

"What? Oh, my goodness. What is it?"

"It's a girl, Mom. Her name is Violet." My mom named all three of her kids after her precious plants: Camellia, Dahlia and Rowan. For nine months of pregnancy, I couldn't find a single name that seemed right, and just like that, my new baby girl's name fell out of my mouth. I'm carrying on a tradition I never thought I even cared about. Maybe I was feeling sentimental talking to my mom, now that I had been a mom for all of thirteen hours. And since I didn't have anyone to consult with to finalise a name, Violet it is.

"No, what is it? What's her *date*?" My mom frantically needing to know the precious answer that will determine whether or not she can form a bond with her first, and likely only grandchild. She rushed past the gender information, didn't care about weight, height, time of birth or how either of us was doing. No, she just wants to know what IT is.

"She's Vita Longas. She'll be seventy-four when she dies, Mom. She's not Rowan."

Chapter Four

Two generations ago, it was decided that we as individuals weren't doing enough to save our planet. Overpopulated, polluted and with climate change causing Mother Nature to fight back with a vengeance, something drastic had to be done. Medicine had advanced so far that people were no longer dying from viruses, diseases or infections. No one had cancer, AIDS or even the flu. The life expectancy was reaching well over one hundred and twenty years and the planet was beyond capacity, so the Governments stepped in and took matters into their own hands. After many years of tribunals, studies and prototypes, The Solution was born. Two scientists, Dr Ignacio Parisi and Dr Paul Malcolm created an invention called the ParColm Vial. A minuscule quarter-inch glass container of potassium chloride that is implanted into the carotid artery of every newborn. It is like a tiny bomb inside your neck that starts ticking down as you take your first breath, counting down the moments, until your last. The vials containing life expectancy are administered randomly, and no amount of money or power can protect you. So, death remains arbitrary, as it always has — except now everyone has a known expiry date, like yoghurt or milk.

There is no rhyme or reason, and when your time is up: boom. But instead of a big blast, it is small and quiet and painful only for your loved ones, the people who have been expecting it all along, but still have to get on with the pain of living. And it isn't like you could live recklessly; death can still find you in the same old ways. People still die in car accidents, get shot, drown or die from suicide.

The Solution didn't happen overnight. At first, people were understandably livid and outraged. Who was the Government to think they could play God? There were years of turmoil and unrest. There were constant riots and assassination attempts on high-level officials. People were out for blood, especially for the doctors who invented this killing contraption. In order to give people back some of their humanity, an ultimatum was reached where people would be given the information in their vial and it was their choice to find out or not what their DD — Death Date — was. With your birth certificate also comes your death certificate. Eventually, people got used to living and dying under The Solution. While it didn't make death any easier, the benefits of having less drain on resources and the planet was worth it.

With the changes, life expectancies were grouped into four categories: Vita Longas, over 75; Vixit Vitam, 30-75; Vita Brevis, under 30; and Vitam Non-Vixit, under 10. Everything is derived from Latin terms, just like names in medicine and nature — but there is nothing natural about predetermined execution. Every culture, religion and family, handles the information of their DDs differently. Some believe in keeping their information a secret, sealing their Death Certificate and never finding out; while others are open and forthright, talking about their Death Date just like they do their Birth Date. Only medical professionals and the authorities who work for The Solution have access to this personal information. An easy scan of a vial can tell exactly how many years, months and days a person has left.

I am one of the lucky ones, at the very top of the age limit with a DD of 80. I was born with time. Insert every cliché quote you've ever heard: seize every moment, live every day to its fullest, be grateful for every sunrise and sunset. It's hard to feel anything but guilty when you are born with something that others weren't. Because my sister isn't as lucky as me and my brother never got a chance. Vitam Non-Vixit: '*a life not lived*'. It's hard to live in the shadow of a ghost.

Chapter Five
Dahlia — DD in 73 years, 10 months, 20 days

It's just before lunch at school. I'm in the second grade. My stomach is hurting and I go to the school nurse. I'm sitting on the crisp white paper sheet on top of the bed in the nurse's office with my skinny pale legs hanging down over the sides. The nurse is standing just outside the door and I can see her holding the phone to her ear and hear the muted sound of ringing over and over. She eventually gives up and looks down at a paper where she must have seen another phone number.

"Hello, Mr Dobbs, I'm calling from Parklane Elementary School. Your daughter Dahlia isn't feeling well and needs to be picked up."

They've called Dad. He wouldn't be too happy about that. He had a big important case at his law firm this week and was worrying about it this morning at breakfast.

"Yes, I understand your wife should be home, sir, but we have tried calling several times and there has been no answer. Yes. Okay, thank you. We'll see you soon."

The nurse comes back in to tell me my dad will be here shortly. I remember thinking it is strange that it is dad instead of mom coming to get me, but I'm excited to see him in the middle of the day. Suddenly, my stomach isn't hurting any more, but I don't want to tell the nurse that because I'm excited to see my dad now. Maybe once we're home, he'll take me for a ride in his old red truck down the back quarter before Camellia gets home from school.

Dad comes into the office in his new suit and he has a serious look on his face. I can tell we're not going to be going for a ride in his truck later. I buckle myself into the backseat of his car and we drive away without him saying much. He's usually so silly and fun in the car, rolling down the windows and listening to music really loudly — but not today. At the stop light, he asks me how I'm feeling and I lie and say that my tummy is hurting a lot. He looks back at me with his sad face and already at seven I can tell he's not really thinking about me. I know that look in his eye, and it's saved just for mom.

As we turn off the highway and turn up onto the long tree-lined road that bends back behind the house, Dad yells out, "Oh, Christ, she's done it again!"

Dad screeches to a stop and tells me to stay inside the car. Scared and confused, I slump down into my seat and pull the seatbelt tighter around me to feel safe and protected by something. I can see Dad running down the freshly mown lawn towards the greenhouse. Off to the side is the special tree mom planted five years ago, with its skinny branches being weighed down by red berries. The ground is so full of squished and stomped-on berries that it looks like tomato juice all over the grass. There is a shovel leaning up against the tree and a big pile of dirt beside it. That's Rowan's tree.

Now Dad is banging on the greenhouse door, yelling for Mom to open it up. He has tears in his eyes as he comes back to the car and takes me into the house and sits me down in front of the TV. He gives me some of the M&Ms he keeps hidden and tells me to stay in the house. After four TV shows, I can hear the school bus down the hill, stopping and dropping off my sister Camellia, who's twelve. It takes her a few minutes to walk up the hill, so I remember hiding the rest of the M&Ms under a pillow so I wouldn't have to share. When she gets inside the house, she yells at me that I'd better be sick because she had to ride on the bus with the smelly O'Neal boy since I wasn't there to sit with her. She comes into the living room and asks where Mom is. I tell her that Daddy picked me up and that Mommy won't come out of the greenhouse. She looks at me and runs around the back side of the house to the window overlooking the yard. She comes back in and sits right close beside me on the couch and just stares straight ahead at the TV and starts biting her nails. We sit like this for a while, watching the commercials on TV. "Camellia, why is there a big pile of dirt by

Rowan's tree? Is Mommy planting something else there?" I ask.

"No, Dahlia. Mommy dug up Rowan's coffin again. She's locked herself in the greenhouse with him."

Chapter Six
Dahlia — DD in 54 years, 9 months, 12 days

"Hello! Oh my gosh, there she is. Ohhh, she's gorgeous!" Into our hospital room walks my sister Camellia, thick brown bob hair swinging effortlessly over her shoulders. She's wearing a crisp button-up Oxford shirt and khaki pants. My sister is always sensibly dressed, like she could be going into a business meeting or on a walking tour of Rome.

"Shhh," I say. "Not so loud!" Just as Violet lets out a whimper from her deep newborn sleep.

"Sorry. Sorry. You know babies aren't really my thing. But I'm such an excited aunt. How are you? Did it hurt? Where's Milo?"

It hurt when I woke up this morning, and Milo had vanished, I think to myself. "He's… not… ummm. Not here. Can you give us a ride home?"

I'm about to break down and tell Camellia the whole story. How the guy I thought was the one, the one who I went ahead and planned a future with, a baby with, has a) left us at the hospital, and b) going to be dead within six months. But then I see the book he'd left us poking out of the bag. "*Trust in me. This is not the end and I will make this right.*" His cryptic message makes me pause and decide to keep things to myself, for at least a little while longer.

"He had to go. But it's okay. We just need a ride home and we'll get settled and I'll figure things out."

"What? Where did he *have* to go? Do you have any idea what you're doing? I thought Milo was the baby guy with all the info."

"He is. But it's mostly instinct anyway, right?" I look my sister straight in the eye, trying to convince myself more than her.

"Was it instinct that told you to put the baby's diaper on backwards?"

***

We hadn't been dating that long. Only about three months, and we were still in that *it's hard to get out of bed because nothing outside is better than what's happening between the sheets,* kind of new romance phase. Until one day I bolted out of bed with a deep cramping pain in my stomach.

"What is it? Are you okay?" he said as he sat up, shirtless, with his toned stomach tanned from our weekend away at the lake.

"No, my stomach really hurts and I feel like I have the flu or something. My head is pounding. I think I need to go to the doctor," I said, hunched over, holding my gut as I tried to find my clothes under a pile of discarded jeans and t-shirts. I reached under the bed and found my underwear — delicate and new, just like this relationship — which had been thrown off in a fit of passion that still caught me by surprise. We'd made love at least once every day since we'd met three months ago, but the desire hadn't even come close to being satiated. This was right around the time things would settle into a familiar routine with my past boyfriends, and this was yet another sign that this one was different. "It's the Monday of the holiday weekend. I won't be able to get into my doctor. Can you drive me to the walk-in clinic?"

After a short drive, Milo let me out at the door to the clinic office and said he'd go find a parking spot and meet me inside. Thankfully, the wait wasn't too long on that scorching hot August day. After giving a urine sample to the nurse, I waited for the doctor to examine me. I was sitting naked from the waist down in a paper dress, half wondering what was taking Milo so long, and half grateful he hadn't found me in here looking like this. There was a quiet knock at the door and I was relieved when a balding middle-aged man with a heavy British accent entered the room. The doctor first typed my information into his computer and then scanned my ParColm Vial. No use going to extreme medical interventions if someone's Death Date is just around the corner.

The doctor got right down to business, and without any introductory pleasantries he gave me my diagnosis.

"Your urine sample was quite cloudy and murky and tested positive for a urinary tract infection. I'll write you a prescription for fourteen days of penicillin and that will clear it right up." With his back to me, typing on the computer, he continued to speak. "And did you know you're pregnant?"

**

I stumbled out of the doors to the clinic, squinting my eyes as they adjusted from the fluorescent lights inside to the piercing August sunlight. I was disoriented, not familiar with this neighbourhood and not able to concentrate on the street names around me. My mind was racing a million miles an hour, but I couldn't seem to put one foot in front of the other. Pregnant? I'm pregnant. How can I be pregnant? I mean, *I know how* — but we had been really careful with protection, hadn't we? I suddenly realised I was feeling light-headed. The intense heat outside and the recently delivered life-changing news had me feeling like I was going to pass out. I slumped myself down onto a bench a couple of steps away and put my head between my legs. I stayed like that for a long time, until I could hear my name being called.

"Dahlia! Dahlia. Oh my gosh, are you okay? I'm sorry I couldn't find a close parking spot, and by the time I got into the office they said you had already left. What is it? What did they say?"

"I think I'm going to be sick," I said, as the words and what was inside my stomach came spewing out onto the sidewalk. I narrowly missed Milo's sneakers and my purse. Milo, unfazed, sat down beside me and started rubbing my back. After a couple of minutes, he found a Kleenex from inside my bag and I cleaned my face off. I sat up straight against the back of the bench next to my boyfriend of three months and realised I was about to change his life forever, too. That thought was enough to make me feel like I could go for round two at decorating the sidewalk; but instead, I looked straight into Milo's auburn brown eyes. He looked so concerned and compassionate, I could feel my stomach starting to unknot. I reached out to hold his hand, needing to feel his strength to give me strength to deliver the words "we're pregnant". Immediately, as I said them, a giant smile spread across his face. He bolted up from the bench and did a little leap in the air. It was such a child-like visceral reaction that I couldn't help but giggle. Then he sat down next to me and pulled me tightly into his chest and I could feel both our hearts pounding. With his face tucked into my neck, he was kissing the side of my head and talking into my ear. "This is incredible news. I'm so happy. You're happy, right, Dahlia? Oh my gosh. Amazing!" He leaned back and clapped his hands together like he was leading a cheer. I was so stunned by his immediate excitement to this news that I couldn't help but smile.

"Of course, yes, it's wonderful. Just a little surprising, right?" I said, looking for some shred of anxiety to cross his face.

"Sure, yes, surprising. Definitely. But I've always wanted to be a dad, and you will be an amazing mom. And I love you, and this is the best news in the world!"

I decided against ruining this moment with all the billions of doubts and questions I had and just tried to absorb some of his genuine thrill in this news.

"What do you need? Should we get you home to rest. God, you are gorgeous. I love you so much." Milo started kissing me all over my arms and face.

"Well, first of all, your gorgeous knocked-up girlfriend needs this prescription filled for her urinary tract infection; and then yes, home sounds good," I said, handing Milo the piece of paper from the doctor as I stood up, avoiding the mess on the sidewalk in front of me. "What a sexy thing I am," I said, looking down and shaking my head at the mess.

"I've never been more attracted to you in my life," Milo said, as he swatted at my behind and grabbed me by the arm, pulling me into his side as we walked down the sidewalk hand in hand.

***

"I wish I could stay with you, but Kane and I have a rally tonight and I really can't miss it." Camellia, always the activist, married a fellow Vita Medium. With just over four decades to live, the two of them chose to focus their lives on The Cause, instead of on a family. And with less than fifteen years left, Camellia's drive and passion towards making a difference and leaving some kind of legacy behind had become an obsession. The Cause is a non-government organisation, like a watchdog that keeps tabs on The Solution, holding it accountable and maintaining the rights of citizens. My sister has always been pragmatic and focused to a fault, and that is exactly who you'd want in the time of crisis; but emotions are not really her thing.

"It's okay, I'm sure Maria will be over soon. She saw us leaving yesterday and will be anxious to meet the baby. Thank you for the ride. Really. You were a life-saver," I say, as I look over at Violet asleep in the car seat that I'd placed on top of my kitchen table. Had she been in there too long? Could she get SIDS from being in a car seat this long? Didn't I read something about that on a pamphlet at the doctor's office? And should she even be up on the table in that seat? What if she wiggled? Could it fall off? My mind is racing through a thousand different catastrophe scenarios. Milo would know the answers to these questions.

"She's beautiful, Dahlia, and you're going to be great. Call me if you need anything. I'll see you next month for Dad." Camellia was already half way out the door as her voice caught saying the word Dad. I'd been in the process of moving Violet's car seat off the table and was once again fiddling around with the straps as the door slammed shut behind her. There was no hug for me or kiss for Violet, but I knew my sister would be here if I needed her.

I finally get the buckle undone and scoop up Violet's warm, snuggly body. Her legs mechanically tuck back up into her torso, the way they'd been positioned inside me for months. I bring her tiny head to my shoulder, careful to support her fragile neck and breathe in her intoxicating smell. I close my eyes to commit it to memory and inhale deeply as tiny feathery hairs at the back of Violet's head tickle my nostrils. We sit together like that for a long time on the couch until Violet's mouth starts making a sucking motion and I am able to feed her without too much finagling and discomfort. We are already both finding our own rhythm together and while she is being fed, I can feel my soul being fed, too. I hadn't been sure I was up for this motherhood thing and can't really think past today about how I'll handle everything on my own; but in this moment, I feel at peace and contented. I know I will over-think every waking moment we'll have together for the next sixty-six years, but in this moment, as she wraps her tiny fingers around my pinky, I whisper to her, "We're going to be okay. Just you and me."

After an hour of cuddling on the couch, I can hear someone coming up the front step. "Knock, knock!" I see Maria's black bun piled on top of her head as she pokes her nose in through the door jamb. A giant toothy smile spreads across her wrinkled face as she spots us on the couch.

"Hello!" I say happily. "Come and meet Violet."

Four years ago, a sweet older couple named Miguel and Maria Lopez moved into the duplex next door. I hadn't made many close connections in the city since my job was all done online, so I'd mostly kept to myself, but Maria and I bonded immediately over my little garden. "You don't often see too many young people tending to a garden these days," Maria said to me over the short chain-link fence, as she was unloading moving boxes into her new home.

"My parents are gardeners. They own a greenhouse. I hated it as a kid, but once I moved to the city, I craved the dirt and greenery. Don't tell my mom," I said with a smile. It's true, my mom would be shocked if she knew I had ever touched soil again. When I left home, I made such a fuss that I wanted concrete, people and noise. I never wanted to watch anything grow ever again.

But the summer I moved into the little post-war six hundred square-foot duplex, I pulled out all the grass in my postage stamp backyard and planted rows of carrots, peas and kale in a small raised garden bed and had half a dozen tomato plants and pots of fresh herbs.

As I got to know Maria and Miguel, I learned they were some of the unfortunate ones whose Death Dates were both later than their children's. They had both been teachers and lived a modest, happy life until, one by one, their children died. Being devoutly catholic, they had chosen never to find out their family members' DDs; but after the last of their four children had passed away, the couple had suffered with enough of the unknown and decided to learn their own fates. Almost poetically, as if the universe was finally taking pity on them, they found out they both had six years left to live and would die within weeks of each other.

With so much loss in their lives, you could always see pain resting just behind their eyes. Maria was a talker and would go into great detail about every one of her children. She said in order to keep their memories alive she needed to speak about them and share all their joys and sadness. "That is the secret to keeping your heart healthy," she would say. This was not something I was used to with my own mother. Not speaking about the dead was how I was raised.

Miguel was an extremely talented woodworker. When I was out in the garden, I would see him in his little workshop, carving the most intricate pieces. It was just a hobby, but he made pretty good money in his retirement selling off his pieces. He confessed to me one day that he wanted to save up and take Maria on a Mediterranean cruise, something special they'd never been able to do before. He was hoping I could help him get the word out about his woodworking. I told him I could do better than that. My job was making websites and that I could make one for him where he could showcase his extraordinary pieces. It didn't take long before he had several high-paying projects lined up and he was thrilled. They were so grateful and wanted to repay me for my time, which I refused, but before long Maria would come by and start tidying up my place and leaving me meals in the fridge. I would be up all night sucked into my online world and forget to eat all day, but I started to count on the fact that if I opened my fridge there would be some home-made enchiladas or pozole. We also started making a regular thing of Sunday night dinners. I was so desperate to leave home all those years ago and be on my own, but it felt nice to be cared for and checked in on.

***

Maria was the one who set Milo and I up. He had been a school friend of her youngest son Oscar. When Milo was coming by one Sunday afternoon to check on the couple, Maria had made a big production about him staying over for dinner and that he should meet their lovely young *single* neighbour. She knew I didn't have much of a social life and that I probably spent far too much time on my computer and socialising with the elderly, so her matchmaker senses were on overdrive. I was reluctant, until she said that she'd shown him what a wonderful job I'd done for Miguel's web page and that he'd been interested to talk more about his own website needs for his art business. I'd just finished my most recent contract and was needing to find some new clients, so I agreed to dinner purely for professional reasons.

That was until I spotted the three of them sitting outside in their backyard drinking beers and laughing. It was his back that I saw first, wide and strong. The cotton fabric from his shirt stretched tightly over his broad shoulders. He was casually dressed in a grey-shirt and jeans and had long wavy brown hair that fell just below his ears. He looked completely relaxed and at ease, like the kind of guy who is so comfortable in his skin that he fits in anywhere. I watched them for ages from my window. I couldn't hear their conversation, but it was clear from their expressions that they jumped between happy memories, with their mouths moving quickly and their faces animated with smiles, to sudden breaks in words where their smiles faded and the hard memories took over and held them in a suspended grief. I watched this back-and-forth dance until suddenly I caught a glimpse of myself in my bathroom mirror and realised my messy ponytail and ripped jeans could use an upgrade. After switching out my glasses for contacts and throwing on a bit of blush to give my pale complexion some life, I spotted the flirty sundress I'd bought on a whim last summer. It had fitted me so well in all the right places, but I had never found the right occasion for it. There was something about the look of that man sitting on the other side of my fence that seemed like this was an evening I wouldn't forget.

I swung open the screen to my back porch, trying to look effortlessly cool, and locked eyes across the fence with a face that somehow looked so new and yet so familiar to me it made my heart skip a beat. I had never seen him before, that I was sure of, but I felt so instantly connected to him.

"Dahlia, this is Milo Paris," said Maria, scanning me up and down and giving me a hidden thumbs-up at the obvious effort I'd put into my appearance.

"Hi, nice to meet you," I said, reaching my hand out to shake his.

"Hello. Maria and Miguel have been telling me all about you," he said, as he stood and pulled out a chair for me to take a seat and stayed standing while Maria and I sat back down. Such a small gesture, but one that did not go unnoticed by either of us women. This is the kind of thing that would normally annoy me. I'm the kind of girl who can pull out her own chair, open her own door and pay her own bills, but something about Milo's authenticity gave me pause to appreciate his chivalry.

Miguel reached down into the cooler and handed me a cold beer and I took a big long swig, aware that all three eyes were staring intently at me.

"I've heard a lot about you, too," I said, after swallowing down my drink. "Maria was telling me all about your art. That you were some kind of prodigy in high school. Something about a big scholarship to a fancy art college."

"Oh, ya. I wish I could say I graduated from that fancy college… but I did attend for a few years. I just found it was stifling my creativity more than inspiring it," Milo said honestly.

"Well, you didn't need that silly degree in the end, did you, Milo?" Miguel let out a chuckle, slapping Milo on the back. "Milo has sold his sculptures all over the world. Huge metal structures. I've never really quite understood them, not much of an eye for that kind of thing, but I hear they're pretty well-received."

It was true; the day before, when Maria felt it necessary to give me the entire biography on their upcoming guest, she'd leaned in behind me at my computer, pointing out different links for me to click on that showed Milo's pieces showcased in galleries and parks all over the world. She'd told me what a sweet, young man he was, always so polite and thoughtful. He'd spent a lot of time at their home after his mother had died in his final year of high school. His father had never been in the picture and he was old enough to live on his own, but just as the Lopez's had done with me, they'd opened their door and hearts to Milo.

"Do you remember those comic books you and Oscar used to make? Oscar would come up with the most absurd and wild scenarios for these action heroes and you would draw it all out. They were incredible. I think I still have one around here somewhere. I'll have to check the basement later," Maria said, leaning back in her chair and smiling.

Milo explained a bit about his artwork and that these days he was focused on the metal sculptures, but he'd started off sketching as a kid and received his scholarship based on his watercolour paintings. He had a studio close to downtown and had a small loft apartment above it. "Sometimes I'll get so immersed in a project that I won't realise what time or day it is even. I'll forget to eat or sleep."

"Dahlia is just like that, aren't you, dear?" Maria said, smiling. "We'll see her lights on all hours of the night. She'll get sucked into that computer of hers and won't come up for air."

The conversation flowed so easily between the four of us. I was surprised I was able to feel relaxed and even flirty in front of Miguel and Maria. I could never imagine having my own parents listening in on a first date. Does this even count as a date, I wondered? Before we'd even started on the main course, I was sure hoping it counted as a date, because I was enthralled by this mystery man.

***

"I think I've probably had enough. I'm not going to be able to drive home," Milo said, as Maria topped up his wine glass. We had all pushed away our plates after a three-hour feast. With our crumpled-up napkins on our laps, Milo's chair and mine had inched closer and closer over the course of dinner until now our legs kept touching under the table.

"Nonsense. It's such a beautiful evening, and we haven't seen you in so long. You can stay in our guest room tonight. We insist. Don't we, Miguel?" Maria said, as she shoved Miguel's chair. His head popped up after he'd been snoozing in his chair for the better part of an hour.

"Ahh, yeah. Stay over. Have another glass," Miguel stammered.

"Now that you're awake, could you help me clear the table, my dear?" Maria said, as she started to load up the plates.

"Let me," Milo said, moving quickly to grab the glasses from the table.

"No, no! You two enjoy the sunset. Please. We've bored you enough with all our old stories," Maria said, as her and Miguel walked up the steps into the back of their house.

I surveyed the table, counting the empty bottles of wine, cans of beer and even a half-finished bottle of Don Julio that Miguel and I had been sipping on. I hadn't been keeping track, but I knew it had been a long time since I'd had this much to drink. With Maria and Miguel inside, Milo turned his body towards mine and put his arm around the back of my chair. "I've had a really good time tonight. I wasn't sure what to expect when Maria told me she wanted me to meet their neighbour. I think she might have used the word recluse." Milo laughed and gave me a push on the shoulder to show he was kidding. This gesture moved his body even closer to mine and we both paused with our faces within inches of each other. "I'd like to see you again, soon," he said.

"I'd like that, too," I said, closing my eyes as we moved in towards each other's mouth. Just then, the screen door flung open with a bang and we both jumped back, surprised.

Maria came back outside and gathered up the rest of the plates. I took another swig of my drink to clear the sexual tension.

"Why don't you take Milo in and show him your computery thing? See what you can do for his business," Maria said innocently in her English-as-a-second-language way.

I choked back my wine, coughing as Milo and I shot each other a smile, with Maria looking at us, confused.

"Sure. Why don't you come in and I can show you some of the sites I've made and you can see if there is anything that would suit your work?"

Milo started up the steps as I grabbed the half-bottle of wine left on the table and our two wine glasses. Maria gave me a very obvious wink and smile. I stumbled as I stood up, not realising the effect of all the afternoon of drinking in the sun had had on me. But I was feeling warm and happy and there was a gorgeous man walking up into my house, which wasn't a common occurrence for me.

If Milo had over-indulged in the drinks as I had, he wasn't showing it. I was holding on to the side of my kitchen table and was trying to stand up straight and focus without showing the amount of effort I was putting into this simple task. He was asking me all sorts of questions about my websites and the clients I've had, as he started moving towards the table to sit down. Before he had a chance, I moved into him and met his lips. We held our mouths still together for a long time at first, feeling the heat swelling up, before exploding into kissing fast and passionately. His tongue found mine and they pushed deep into each other's mouths hard and fast. If I was feeling dizzy before from the alcohol, the room was positively spinning now. He grabbed the sides of my waist and lifted me up onto the table, straddled between my legs. His hands were circling all over the bare skin on my back, sending shivers deep down my legs. I let out a deep sigh and laid myself down onto the table. It was not like me to be so forward, especially after just meeting, but I'd had some liquid courage and I was caught up in the look of desire in his eyes, which gave me the nerve to pull him on top of me. I could feel his bodyweight heavy and hot on me, but this feeling only lasted a second before he stood back up and moved away from the table.

"What is it? What's wrong?" I said, slurring my words, unsure if I was drunk from the mixture of alcohol we'd consumed that evening or the taste of his mouth.

"Uhh, sorry. I just don't feel right about this. I don't want to rush things," he said, as he smoothed down his t-shirt over the top of his chiselled stomach muscles.

"I understand. I guess we got a little carried away. Not the kind of business I was supposed to be showing you, right?" I said with an awkward laugh, trying to lighten the mood with a joke. I was not sure if I'd been rejected entirely or had just been given a very polite rain check. I was really hoping it was the latter, so to try and save the situation I attempted to steer things back into the professional realm.

"Let me go get my laptop and I'll show you some examples of my past sites."

When I finally got into my bedroom and closed the door, I stared at myself in the mirror and saw a blurry, buzzy reflection of myself. My eyes were only open half way and my mouth was red and swollen from our kissing. I put my hand up to my heart to steady it from beating so fast. I laid down on my bed to try and catch my breath and sober up a bit before I went back out there. And then I closed my eyes. Just for a second.

***

I woke up in a mess of sheets and pillows with my laptop stuck to the bare skin on my thigh. I rolled over and saw the clock blinking at me — 6.48am. What day is it? I squinted my burning eyes, realised I still had my contacts in and felt a throbbing in my head. As I propped myself up against the headboard, I looked down at myself and saw a crumpled yellow sundress splattered with red wine stains. Milo! I started to remember the night before. The long, drawn-out meal with Maria and Miguel. The making out on the table and then coming into my room to get my computer. But I must have fallen asleep. I never did come back out. Oh my god! I passed out and left that man alone in my kitchen. I hope he didn't come in and find me sprawled out fully clothed, drooling on my bed. I was mortified. He must have gone back over to Maria and Miguel's and slept there. I went into the bathroom and started running the shower, and was sure I'd never see that beautiful face again. There was no way he was going to have anything to do with me romantically again, and he's for sure not hiring me to make his website. As the hot water ran down my skin, it burned on my shoulders that had been bare in the sunshine the day before, further reminding me of the bad choices I'd made that day. Not wearing sunscreen was the least of them.

I slipped on the ripped jeans that I'd discarded the day before when I changed into my dress, and threw on a white t-shirt. I put my hair up in a wet bun, finally took out my contacts, put on glasses and brushed the red wine stains off my teeth. Feeling moderately better, I opened my bedroom door to the smell of coffee. Stunned, I turned back around and closed the door behind me with my back pressed against it. Oh god! Coffee. He must still be here and he's made coffee, I thought. I frantically looked around my room, deciding whether I should comb out my hair or put on some make-up, but I realised he could have heard the door open and close and I didn't think I had time. I thought I might as well face the music as myself — it's not like I had much to lose at that point.

I sheepishly walked down the hallway and turned into the kitchen to see the coffee pot filling up, but there was no one there. I looked around for clues, but there was no note, no shoes and no indication anyone had ever been here, other than the coffee brewing. As I reached to grab a cup from the cupboard, I could hear footsteps coming up the front steps. I turned around to see the same auburn eyes I had been drowning in the night before, coming in through the front door.

"Hi," he said with a smile on his face. "I hope I didn't wake you banging around the kitchen this morning." He was carrying a brown paper bag I recognized from the twenty-four-hour corner store a block away. "I wanted to make us something for breakfast, but you don't really have any food, other than what looks like all of Maria's leftovers and a lot of garden vegetables."

"Yeah, I don't really cook much these days," I said, as I reached out to help him unload the bag. He'd bought eggs, tomato sauce, sausages, and a toothbrush.

"I wanted to make a good first impression this morning. A second first impression, I guess," he said, as he smiled and grabbed the toothbrush from my hand and threw it in the back pocket of his jeans.

"You made a great first impression," I said. "I'm the one who passed out," I blurted out, avoiding his eyes. "Did you go back to Maria and Miguel's last night?"

"No, I just slept on your couch," he said, as he motioned over to my narrow beige couch with a small quilt neatly folded up over the back. "I didn't want you to wake and think I'd just left. And I wanted to be nearby in case you needed something. I wasn't sure what condition you were in."

"That couldn't have been very comfortable. I'm so sorry. I just got carried away last night. I was having such a good time and…"

He cut me off and pulled me in for a kiss, and I was already forgetting what it was I was apologising for.

"Now sit down and relax. I'm going to make you baked eggs," he said, as he pulled out a chair for me and poured me that much-anticipated cup of coffee. I watched as he started moving around the kitchen effortlessly, pouring tomato sauce into a sizzling frying pan and opening the carton of eggs. When I commented on his skills, he told me he learned it all from his mom. They spent a lot of time cooking together when he was little, but then he had to do most of it on his own when he got older. I noticed his posture changed dramatically when he mentioned his mother. His shoulders folded in and his stance became almost child-like as he inhaled deeply and then changed the subject.

We both sat down to eat and I raved about how delicious it was, and we talked about the similarities in both our careers, being self-employed and how important creativity was to us. We drank two full pots of coffee as the conversation flowed so easily and the time flew by. There was so much electricity in the air that I could feel myself starting to get warmer and flushed. He must have felt the same thing. When there was finally a break in our chatting, I saw that same look in his eye that got me into trouble the night before, but this time it was his turn to make the move.

"Now where were we last night?" he said, as he gently pushed me back down on top of the table. My legs were dangling over the end and my arms were held down above my head by his strong biceps. He started feverishly kissing my lips and moved down my throat and neck. His one hand let go of my arms and slid up under my t-shirt and under my bra. He caressed my breast and circled around my nipple, pulling it gently as I let out a deep moan. With both hands, he started to unbutton my jeans and shimmied them down my legs and they dropped to the floor. He reached his fingers up under my lacy thong and felt around tenderly inside of me. Our kissing continued and I was biting his lips to keep from crying out in pleasure. He grabbed me from underneath and wrapped my legs around his torso and carried me down the hallway into my room, dropping me onto my bed. We rolled around in the covers, kissing and touching every part of each other. His muscles wrapped around on top of me and I felt the length of him pressed against my thigh. He locked eyes with mine and his kisses became deeper and longer and he pushed himself into me. He went in slowly at first and then faster as I gripped the bed post behind me.

And that was the beginning of the end. We barely spent a day apart after that. Both our jobs had us working at odd hours, but any time we weren't working, we were together. We moved between each other's homes, depending on the day, but often would always end up back at my place on Sundays for dinner with Miguel and Maria. Maria was so proud of herself for being such a terrific matchmaker, and I had to admit I finally felt settled into the life I had always hoped for myself. I had people I cared for and who cared for me in the city I felt most at home. I had my dream job and I was starting to fall in love.

***

Maria is sitting on the couch with Violet lying on her lap. She's bending down and kissing her bare toes, saying, "This little piggy went to the market…" I can see a smile on Violet's face, and while Milo's baby books would have said it's just gas at this age, I'd prefer to believe that Violet has already fallen in love with Maria. I had just taken a much-needed shower after our return from the hospital and was unpacking in the kitchen when the question I knew was coming is asked.

"Where's Milo, Dahlia?" Maria asks from the couch. "Did he have some spurt of creativity after Violet's birth that he just had to capture at his studio?" Milo did have a tendency to vanish now and then in the middle of dinner or cancel on plans if he felt a moment of inspiration. It was an annoying habit that I'd gotten used to over the past year; one Milo had assured me he'd try his best to curb once the baby was born.

"Not quite," I say painfully. "He left us, Maria. He was there for her birth, but when I woke up later that day he was gone. I don't know where he is." I'm about to tell Maria about his newly revealed Death Date, but the look of horror on her face of just the news that he was gone was painful enough. She'd also suffered enough loss, and if Milo has six more months to live, that was longer than Maria has, so I didn't want to upset her even more knowing she'd have to deal with another death in her lifetime. "Maybe he was overwhelmed or maybe he's just an asshole. I don't really know. He seems to be repeating the common male trait in his family of being a deadbeat dad like his dad and grandpa," I say harshly; "but he wins the award for skipping out the fastest. Leaving while we're still in the hospital is impressive." Now both Maria and I are crying. She pulls me in and holds me tightly, apologising over and over.

"I'm so sorry, my darling. I am just so shocked. This is not the Milo I know. He was so excited to be a father and he loves you so much. I just don't understand." As we cry, we both take turns cuddling Violet, her warm little body filling an emotional void in both of us. Maria assures me that whatever I need, her and Miguel will help. "I know we don't have much time left…," she sobs into my shoulder, thinking about their deaths in the fall, "but we're here for you now, however you need us."

"Thank you, Maria. I really don't know what I would do without you," I say. "Actually, there is one thing you could help with now. Would you watch Violet for a couple of hours? There is some pumped breast milk in the fridge if she gets hungry. Milo's phone is turned off, so I haven't been able to reach him at all, but I do have a key to his studio. I want to go and see what I can find out."

***

Milo's studio loft is usually a leisurely thirty-minute walk from my house along the river towards downtown, but after having gone through labour just the day before, I decide that taking the bus is the more sensible option. After a couple of stops I get off and walk the familiar street lined with mostly industrial shops and small businesses. I stop in front of a big metal hinged door and reach in my bag for the key to Milo's studio, noticing the empty driveway beside me where his car would normally be parked. I heave open the door, pushing it to the right, exposing the dark, damp room to sunlight. I notice on the floor under the antique mail slot a couple of business-looking letters and a grocery store flyer. I glance through them quickly and without skipping a beat I decide to shove them into my bag. Mail fraud is about the least of my concerns at this point.

I walk over to Milo's desk and scan the paint samples, charcoal pencils, bills, receipts, and a half-finished cup of coffee. Hanging on the wall there is a cork bulletin board and pinned up is a piece of pink paper I recognise as the paperwork from the hospital. On one side is information on the care of newborns: recommended bathing temperature, diaper rash remedies, common baby ailments etc... On the other side is a sketch of me and Violet asleep in the hospital, done in blue ballpoint pen. Written underneath is one line.

D — I'll fix this

I want to tear the page down and rip it into a million pieces. I fight the urge to destroy it, thinking this might be the only time Violet will ever be in her father's art and that it will matter to her some day. I decide to leave the paper pinned up since I don't trust myself to be gentle with it just yet. I make my way upstairs to the open-air loft above. It's just a small galley kitchen, bathroom and bed. I notice the drawers have been rummaged through and Milo's suitcase is gone. Back downstairs, I start to tear apart Milo's shelves and desk.

Tucked behind the desk I find a small box full of children's books. I assume these are books that Milo had got for Violet, so I decide to take them with me. I open up all the drawers and throw in my bag all the files and notebooks from inside the desk. Maybe I'll find something that will give me a clue to his whereabouts.

Feeling light-headed, I sit down on the big brown leather chair beside the desk. I haven't been on my feet for this long since Violet's delivery, and I'm suddenly not feeling so good. As I lean back in the chair to rest, I start to think back to the first night I spent here. We'd been at my place every day for a week after that first night, when Milo woke up one morning after having a crazy dream about some underwater bridge thing. He was describing it to me and grabbed a piece of paper from my desk and started sketching abstract lines and three-dimensional columns. He was completely zoned out when I offered to make us some breakfast. "Uh, no thanks. I'm okay. I need to get home, Dahl. I have an idea for a piece and I have to get working on it." He looked up at me and could likely see both my fascination at his intensity and disappointment that we'd be parting ways after the incredible week we'd had. "You can come with me if you want. I might not be the best host. I tend to get sucked into my bizarre world, but you could bring your laptop and work from my desk if you want." While we'd gotten to know each other so well over the past week, there was still so much that was a mystery to me. I was excited to see the illustrious studio I'd imagined in my head and see where this beautiful man lived and worked.

I was surprised to find Milo lived so close by, but he was in a part of town I'd never spent too much time. His loft ticked off all the boxes of what I'd imagined for a bachelor artist; it was almost a cliché. His workspace was a mess of different paints and pencils, big industrial metal objects and welding equipment. Other than the cluttered desk and bookshelf, there was a big brown leather chair in an otherwise empty room. Upstairs, none of the furniture really matched, but it was much cleaner and more organised than the studio. After a quick tour, Milo left me upstairs while he went down to his desk to start sketching. I worked for a few hours, but I didn't have anything pressing and I was really just passing the time. I had a little nap and then surfed around the web for a while and responded to a few emails, but by 5pm I was bored. Milo had been down in his studio for seven hours and he hadn't even acknowledged me upstairs. I'd leaned over the loft railing several times to try and get a peek at what he was doing. At first, he was sitting with his legs hanging over the armrest of the leather chair, feverishly sketching on a giant pad of paper. Later, I saw him at an easel painting some diagonal lines in black and brown paint. At one point he had even pulled out some modelling clay. I had given up trying to get his attention by clearing my throat or humming. I laid down on his bed and saw my overnight bag I'd quickly packed when we left my house earlier. I remembered the sexy red negligee I'd thrown in at the last minute. I think it's time for a break, I smiled to myself as I put on the lingerie. I'd lived in jeans and t-shirts all week and hadn't had a reason to dress up for Milo, which was one of the best parts of this new relationship. He seemed happy with me at my most comfortable, and while the lacy strings on the thong underwear and the zig-zagging fabric across my body up to the cleavage-baring bra were anything but comfortable, I did think it was time to spice things up a bit.

I walked down the stairs on tip-toes to mimic the effect of wearing high heels. I had to admit I was feeling pretty good about myself, excited to surprise Milo in my outfit. He had his back to me at his easel, so I had to let out a small cough to get his attention. He turned around and saw me in all my red lace glory and looked more in shock than pleasure.

"Hi," he said reluctantly.

"I thought it might be time for a break," I said in my most sultry voice, leaning up against the leather chair.

"Oh, huh. Umm, you look amazing, but I can't really stop right now. I'm kind of in the middle of something. I'm sorry," he said, brushing the hair back from his forehead.

"Sure, I get it," I said, trying not to seem as surprised and disappointed as I really was. "I'm going to go get something to eat, then," I said, as I grabbed my jacket off the side of the chair. It's a long trench-style and luckily covers up all but my humiliation.

"I'm really sorry, Dahlia," he said quickly, as he returned his attention back to the canvas in front of him.

"Can I bring you back anything?" I said, as I slipped on my runners.

"Um, what's that? Uh, no thanks," he said, already distracted.

I slid closed the big metal door and walked out into the warm summer night. I felt frustrated and rejected and suddenly very hungry. I walked for several blocks before I found a little hipster diner. I headed inside and ordered Eggs Benedict and a side of French Fries. No use worrying about how I looked in that outfit any more, so I ordered the greasiest, bloatiest meal on the menu with bitter satisfaction. It took a long time for my food to come, but I was in no rush to get back, so I started reading the newspaper left beside me. The front page of the paper had a picture of the rally that Kane and Camellia's firm had organised the night before. I read over the headline, 'Rebels without a Cause', and scrolled through, trying to see if my sister or brother-in-law were mentioned in the article at all:

The Solution's anti-thesis "The Cause" was out in full force yesterday afternoon, drumming up support and voicing their concerns over the alleged violation of Section 7 in the Solution's Licence of Rights. When asked for comment, Camellia Dobbs-Montgomery, head legal chair for The Cause, was unwavering in her

accusations towards The Solution's potential wrong-
doings. "Those of us at The Cause have a duty as the
watchdog of The Solution to ensure that our citizens'
civil liberties are not violated as The Solution carries
out their activities. There has been speculation that
several high-ranking officials within The Solution's
organisation have been in contact with foreign
bureaucrats interested in purchasing the data retrieved
from expired ParColm Vials. We have always been
assured by The Solution that all information is
confidential and sealed with the highest of security
clearance. Either our sources are wrong, which I doubt,
or there has been a breach somewhere in The Solution's
process, and we at The Cause are following the proper
protocol through filing an injunction to have this
investigated through all the proper channels. If that
fails, we will take matters into our own hands."

***

After I'd finished up at the restaurant, I decided to take
the long walk back to Milo's along the river. It was such
a beautiful evening, with people out walking their dogs
and patios full of people. I turned onto Milo's street and
took a deep breath, swallowing down my earlier
rejection once again. As I started to push open his door,
it swung open forcefully from inside, with Milo
standing shirtless and flushed.

"Where have you been? You've been gone forever!" He closed the door and pushed me up against it, feverishly kissing down my neck and undoing the belt on my jacket as it fell to the ground. I was barely able to get a word out before he was kissing me deeply on the mouth.

"I was taking my time at the restaurant. I thought you were busy." I tried to sound annoyed, but I was already heating up and couldn't hide my enthusiasm.

"I was. But then I wasn't. And I needed you," he said, as he pushed me onto the leather chair. He knelt down on the ground in front of me and kissed my neck and chest and all the way down over my stomach and on top of my panties. He pulled them aside and continued kissing and licking as I writhed in the chair, digging my nails into the leather. His intensity was stronger than ever before and I cried out his name over and over. Just when I thought I couldn't take it any longer, he dropped his pants to the ground and with one arm he scooped me up until he was sitting and I was straddling him. He guided my body onto him with his arms on either side of my thighs. I could tell he was enjoying the view of me in this lingerie while I rode up and down with my chest bouncing in front of him. We both finished at the same time and I fell onto his chest in exhaustion. We lay like that for a while, both catching our breath.

"Sorry about earlier. I'm so used to being alone when I'm working. I kind of get in the zone and can't get out of it," he said, as he stroked his fingers up and down my bare back.

"I understand. I don't really get your whole process, but I can respect you need space to create. I'm like that, too, I guess." We eventually made our way upstairs and Milo laid with me until I fell asleep, before he returned back downstairs to work. I felt him crawl into bed just before sunrise and curled myself into his warm body. We both slept until late the next morning and made love again when we woke up. That time it was slow and thoughtful, not the rushed excitement of the night before, but just as satisfying.

As I sit in the same leather chair, remembering the passion and love that was just beginning for us that day, I have to force myself not to cry. I'm so confused about what has happened and feel so lonely in this big empty room and in this big empty life that we were meant to share. But I have to remind myself I'm not alone. I have to get back to Violet. As soon as my thoughts turn to her, I can feel the milk starting to come. I grab the box I have thrown together of Milo's mysterious life and lock the door behind me. By the time I reach the bus stop, I am leaking milk all down my front. Big wet circles stain my shirt and I don't even bother to conceal them. I am carrying so much pain and betrayal hidden just under the surface, but the greatest love I do have in my life needs me and is reminding me in a not-so-subtle way with a stained t-shirt. "I'm coming, sweetheart," I say to myself, as I board the bus back to my house and my baby.

Chapter Seven
Milo — DD in 0 years, 6 months, 2 days

I'm headed south. I've been driving for two days and have pulled over a few times to sleep, but I need to keep moving. My plan was to settle in somewhere a few hours away, far enough that no one knows me and no one will find me, except now I get the feeling I'm being followed. When I was pulling out of a gas station last night, I saw the same dark grey sedan I'd seen the day before. I didn't stick around long enough to get a good look at the people in the vehicle: just a couple of guys in suits, but something about them gave me an unsettled feeling. I have been driving all day now and taking abrupt turns off the highway to throw off any tracks. I just can't take any chances.

I'd always had this fear in the back of my mind that I would find myself in this situation, but I was on my own so I never worried too much about it; but now I have people who are counting on me — finally I am part of a family. I can't think about that. If I had stayed, I would have just caused more hurt and pain. This is my lot in life, and the sooner I accept it the better. Everyone is better off without me.

Chapter Eight
Dahlia — DD in 54 years, 9 months, 12 days

I don't know what I was expecting for my first evening at home with my baby, but I definitely pictured Milo doting on us both hand and foot. He would have been ordering in food from my favourite place, changing diapers, adjusting nursing pillows and fawning over Violet. He would have insisted I take one of those sitz baths of Epsom salts the doctor mentioned and shift on and off with me for baby duty while I rested as much as possible. Instead, our reality looks a little bit different. I am still being greatly cared for in the form of Miguel and Maria, and while I desperately need their help right now, I really do just want to be alone to stare at Violet and cry. Maybe it's for the best I can't do that right now. I can't break down because if I fall apart, I don't know if I can pick myself back up again.

When I return home from Milo's loft, Maria is in the kitchen, stirring something that smells delicious on the stove, while Violet is wrapped up like a tiny mummy in a laundry basket cushioned with blankets on the floor. "I couldn't get that fancy bassinet in your bedroom figured out. It kept collapsing on me. All of my children spent the first six months of their lives sleeping in one of these, and they turned out just fine." I can't argue with her. Violet looks like a peaceful little angel, eyes twitching as she dreams; but within minutes of me coming in the door, as if she can sense her food supply is near, Violet starts crying out from the laundry basket. I nurse her for what feels like the hundredth time today and feel frustrated that she's not getting enough milk, or maybe I'm not making enough. She keeps unlatching, and her cries get louder and more panicked.

"She might not be hungry. I did just give her a bottle of your pumped milk about an hour ago."

"Shhh, shhh, it's okay, sweetheart," I say, as I try and bounce to soothe her. "Do you think it's gas?"

"I don't know, love. You could try giving her a bath. That might calm her down."

I'm sure Maria could see the fear in my eyes. How do I know if the temperature is right? What if I burn her? How can I keep a hold of a tiny slippery body? Did we even buy a baby bathtub?"

"The first time is always daunting. I remember. Here, let's do it together in the kitchen sink." Again, Maria to the rescue!

After Violet's bath, she calms right down and falls fast asleep in my arms. Miguel comes over and joins us for a delicious, yet uncomfortable meal. All three of us trying to make awkward small talk to avoid the elephant in the room in the form of the missing Milo at the head of the table. I manage to scarf down my entire meal with one hand, a skill I didn't know I had until I had a sleeping baby in one arm.

"Why don't I take Violet into your bedroom for a little bit? I'll rock her and see if I can get her down in that bassinet again. That should give you a couple of hours off duty. You need to take it easy, love." Maria manages to scoop up Violet without a peep: she just crinkles up her toes and then stretches right back into blissful slumber. Miguel begins to do the dishes, and while I know I should take a load off, I look around the living room at everything that has just been dropped since coming home from the hospital. I pick up my purse and remember the mail I'd taken from Milo's studio. With Miguel occupied at the sink, I open up the letter that simply says **Mr Milo Paris, Urgent** on the front of the envelope.

Dear Mr Paris,

We have been made aware of the recent changes in your life and need to meet with you urgently to discuss the next steps.

Please get in touch with us at your earliest convenience. We are expecting your call. 1-800-777-9999

Sincerely,

The Resolution

a subsidiary of The Solution

100 1st Avenue, The Core

Recent changes? What changes? That Milo has skipped town. Why would anyone at The Solution, or its subsidiary — some branch I've never heard of called The Resolution — care that Milo is missing? The letter is dated the morning after Violet was born. Milo was in the hospital the night before and must have rushed home, packed up his stuff and left. There is no postage on the letter, so it had to have been hand delivered, and the deliverer must have just missed Milo.

From the stool at the island, I yell over the top of the water Miguel is running, "Hey, Miguel, have you ever heard of The Resolution? Something to do with The Solution?" Miguel turns off the tap and throws a dishcloth over his shoulder as he turns around to face me. I push the letter underneath a stack of other papers, out of sight.

"Umm, let me think. No, doesn't sound familiar. I know they had all sorts of branches when they were just starting out, all with vague threatening-sounding names, but over the years it all just got dissolved into The Solution. Why?"

"Oh, no reason. Something Camellia mentioned the other day," I say to cover myself from more questions about Milo's mail.

"Resolution… hmm. Not The Resolve? I do know about that one. That was another branch. Heinous stuff." Miguel shakes his head.

"What was The Resolve?" I ask Miguel.

"I don't want to upset Maria. She can't hear me telling you. It's too painful for her to relive."

"Oh. Really? Okay, well, she's still in with Violet. I can see the door closed from here," I say, my curiosity hoping he'll fill me in.

Miguel comes over to the island and sits down on the stool next to me. He leans in very closely and is almost whispering as he starts to talk. "Back when The Solution was just starting out and implementing the vial system, there was a lot of backlash. It took a long time for people to come to terms with it all, and The Solution had to take some extreme measures. Understandably, some people were strongly opposed to the entire thing, and those people were dealt with very harshly. No one trusted The Solution at first, and people were scared and outraged by the short life expectancies they were receiving — and when loved ones started dying... well, you can imagine it was anarchy. To deal with the rebels, they created a team called The Resolve. They investigated any signs of defiance against The Solution and penalised to the full extent of their power... execution!" Miguel continues sombrely. "Maria's older brother, Manuelo, was a rural veterinarian. He and his family had a ranch outside the city where they would rehabilitate horses and other sick animals on their property. Well, to make a long tragic story short, Manuelo was opposed to what The Solution was doing, and with his medical training, although on animals, he took matters into his own hands, literally. Now, you have to remember this was long before the ParColm Vials had sensors built in them, so Manuelo figured out how to remove vials from people's necks. It was an excruciatingly painful experience with a terrible recovery process, but people were desperate. Now, you couldn't just have a vial removed and go back to your normal life. For one, the scarring left behind was very obvious, and what if you were ever scanned? You would be killed instantly for subversion. Therefore, Manuelo's services also included relocation to his property. He started a kind of commune where his patients could live, contribute and hide from The Solution and the rest of the world. He begged Maria to join him, but she refused. She's always been so righteous and honest. She loved her brother dearly and knew his heart was in the right place, but this was not a sustainable plan. He must have had at least two dozen people living on his property by the time it all came to an end." Miguel looks off in a distant stare. I get up and turn on the kettle. As I start to make us tea, I'm hopeful Miguel will finish the story quickly before Maria returns. "We never found out how they got caught. There were lots of rumours after that someone left the property and was discovered missing a vial, which led The Resolve back to the ranch. They didn't do follow-up investigations on cases like these. There were hundreds of similar ones back then, but in the end The Resolve's no-holds-barred approach proved to be stronger than people's desire to revolt. Eventually, less and less people were rebelling, until most everyone accepted The Solution's way of doing things. That's why you don't really hear about any of those other groups any more."

"What groups?" Maria says, as she walks into the kitchen.

"Oh, uh… some rally for The Solution Camellia was involved in. I was just asking Miguel if he'd heard of The Resolution," I say quickly, before Miguel has a chance to come up with a lie.

"Resolution. Doesn't ring a bell. Resolve I've heard of." Maria looks Miguel straight in the eyes and my blood runs cold, thinking she's overheard us. "But that branch closed down a lifetime ago." Maria lets out a small sigh and shifts her shoulders back as if she's sloughing off a heavy weight. "Violet fell right asleep. That bath must have been just what she needed. You should get some sleep, too, while you can. We'll leave you girls. Please call me if you need anything tonight. I'm sure it won't be very restful, but I'll be back in the morning to check on you." Maria leans in and gives me a kiss on my forehead and takes Miguel's hand as they walk towards the door.

"Thank you both so much. I don't know what I would do without you!" I say, as the words catch in my throat. Exhaustion and emotions are bubbling at the surface.

"It's our pleasure," Miguel says with a wink, as he puts his arm around his wife's shoulders and shuts the door behind them.

Instead of heading straight to bed, like I know I should, I flip open my laptop and type in the words "Manuelo Veterinarian Solution", and sure enough several articles appear, each one more descriptive and horrific than the last. Sentences jump off the screen one after the other, and I'm so relieved Maria didn't hear us talking about her brother. I click between headlines: *Rabble-rousing Animal Doc Brought to Justice*, *Solution Blasts Vet-Camp*, and begin to read:

Non-Compliance Commune Goes Up in Smoke
An estimated twenty-seven people were killed in a bomb blast on a rural property forty-five kilometres south of the city. The owner of the property, Dr Manuelo Martinez, a well-respected Veterinarian, was allegedly removing ParColm Vials from his acquaintances, as well as housing the rebels on his land. Aerial photographs taken three years before Tuesday's incident show two large barn-like structures on the property, along with several smaller buildings believed to be bunk houses. It is unclear exactly how many people perished, but one neighbour told Q1 News he thought at least twenty people were living and working there, many of whom were women and children. The Solution has taken full responsibility for the attack and no investigation will be undertaken. A comment released to the media from The Resolve, the branch of The Solution that handles any defiance with ParColm Vials, reads: "As stated in The Solution's Statement of Order, article 2a) The Solution has a zero-tolerance

policy for any persons tampering with ParColm Vials. This offence is punishable by death."

By the time I've finished my Internet search, my tea has gone cold and I am numb thinking about what poor Maria has been through. I can't imagine losing a sibling that way. No wonder Miguel didn't want her overhearing. As I pour my tea down the drain, I remember how this whole Resolve story came up in the first place: I was asking about Milo's letter and The Resolution. Just as I'm about to pull out my computer again, I hear a small cry from my bedroom. So much for that rest I was supposed to take. Violet needs me now.

Chapter Nine
Dahlia — DD in 54 years, 7 months, 21 days

Violet's first month went by in a blur. Between all-night feeding sessions and endless diaper changes, we somehow got through it. I could not have done it without Maria, who would come by in the mornings and let me get some rest. She'd often find both me and the baby sprawled out on the couch where we'd been all night, since Violet's days and nights were completely mixed up. "Circadian rhythm," I could just hear Milo explaining the concept to me in his adorable baby encyclopedia voice. I was so overwhelmed with the idea of just being pregnant that he said my job was just to grow our little baby and keep myself healthy, and that he would learn everything there was to know and that he'd share it all with me when we needed it. This was a wonderful notion to my overwhelmed pregnant self at the time, but in our current situation it was horrendous. Thankfully, as a mother of four, Maria knew exactly what to do to soothe Violet and keep me sane. She told me how she'd suffered from postpartum depression with her youngest son and wanted to make sure I had the support I needed. Usually, after a couple of hours' nap and a shower, I felt like myself again and longed to have Violet back in my arms. As days and nights passed by in a haze, there would be moments of pure bliss where Violet would smile or grab my finger and my heart would explode with happiness. Other days I was completely overwhelmed and angry. Angry at Milo for betraying us, and angry at myself for falling for him so quickly and not knowing him as well as I thought. But I didn't have much time to dwell on my pain with a newborn to keep me busy.

And now it was May. This month had been on my mind and my family's mind for my entire life. This is the month my dad dies. I was only eighteen months old when Rowan died, and other than my grandpa, I haven't had much experience with death yet. My dad has always been more of the 'get on with the business of living instead of worrying about the dying' type of guy. Maybe because my mom always did all the worrying about death, or maybe it's because he is the one going first. Well, not first. That was Rowan. Then Grandpa, then Dad; then it will be Camellia and then Mom, and then me. I'll be the one burying my entire family. The "lucky one", as I have always been referred to. Some luck.

My dad has always been content with the vial he was given. He said that fifty-five years was a good amount of time to get out of life what he wanted. My dad, Mr Glass-Half-Full. I wonder if he was always this way, or if the loss of his young son and the crumbling of his wife's mental state forced him to take on this overly optimistic outlook on life? Maybe he became this way for the sake of me and Camellia, so we could count on one parent to be sunshine when the other one could turn to a dark thunderstorm in a split-second.

So now, as I pack up a suitcase full of baby onesies and bottles, along with a black dress for myself and the rest of my clothes for a month's stay at the acreage, I think back to the last time I had this suitcase out, for the reverse trip, where I was leaving them all behind and heading out to the city on my own. I'd made this move hastily, hurting many feelings on my way out. Some relationships have been mended effortlessly over the years, but some have been a much harder journey.

***

Maria and Miguel are out in the driveway, helping Camellia and Kane load up his Volvo with all our bags and baby items. Maria is rocking Violet from side to side, singing a sweet song under her breath. They leave on their two-month Mediterranean cruise at the end of the week. I was so grateful when they changed their plans after they found out I was pregnant, and even more grateful they pushed the dates again after Milo's disappearance.

Maria wipes away tears as she buckles in Violet's car seat and closes the door. She pulls me in tightly and hugs me, while kissing my cheeks over and over. "You travel safe and take care of that little girl. We'll be sending you lots of love… I can't" — she stifles back a cry — "I can't. I have to go inside." Poor Maria. She has had so many goodbyes in her lifetime that she can't seem to bear them any more. Even the short ones, where we will return to one another in just a couple of months. As she makes her way back inside their home, Miguel gives me a tight hug and hands me a book.

"I just finished this novel and it was pretty good. Thought maybe it could distract you while you're gone." I have never seen Miguel read in the entire time I have known him, but I think it's a sweet gesture and I toss the book into my bag.

"Oh, thank you, Miguel. You two have a wonderful time on your cruise. I can't wait to hear all about it. Love you." I buckle in for the two-hour drive home, listening to Kane and Camellia discussing work. I am happy when the conversation doesn't get directed to the back seat with questions about Milo missing.

***

Milo and I had been dating for a month when Camellia insisted, I bring over this mystery man for dinner. Her and Kane lived in a condo an hour away, near The Core and The Solution headquarters. I found it adorable when Milo called to ask what he should wear. I had yet to see him waver in his confidence on any occasion, so I thought this was a good sign that he was putting so much effort into meeting my family. When he picked me up with a bouquet of flowers in the driver's seat, I was touched that he'd been so thoughtful and felt bad when I had to break the news to him. "The flowers are lovely, but I'm going to take them into my place and get them into water. Camellia is NOT a flower kind of girl. Some parts of growing up with a family-run greenhouse have left irreversible damage. This is just one of her quirks."

"Oh, shoot! Well, I'm glad you told me! Any other quirks I should be aware of?"

"Tons, but we don't have time to go through them all now. Let's stop at the liquor store down the street and pick her up some whiskey. That's more her style."

Once we made it inside and the formal introductions were out of the way, I was pleasantly surprised when everyone was getting along so well. I'd always found Kane to be a bit hard to connect with, but it turns out he had an art history minor in college, so he and Milo hit it off right away. I was helping Camellia clear away the dishes in the kitchen after the sushi she'd ordered in from one of the high-end restaurants nearby. I'd never had a single meal at her house and was surprised her pristine modern glass kitchen even had dishes. "I like him, Dahl. He seems really cool. Different from some of the other guys you've dated," Camellia said.

"Yeah, he is, isn't he? I'm glad you like him."

"Where is he from? Have you met his family?"

"No, he doesn't really have any. He moved here when he was a kid. His mom died when he was a teenager. He doesn't really talk about that stuff much."

"Oh," Camellia said with a concerned look in her eyes.

"What? Do you think that's bad that he doesn't want to talk about his past and stuff? Maybe it's really painful."

"No; I guess it's fine. It's still early on. Have you talked about yours? It's not like we had mother-of-the-year. We've got some stuff in our past that's not ideal."

"That's an understatement! No, we haven't really gotten into all that mess yet. Guess we should, hey?" I sighed, acknowledging this thought I've had for a while.

Camellia and I joined the men in the living room and sat down on big abstract metal chairs that looked like they've never been sat in, and I understood why, when I couldn't get comfortable. I ended up sitting with one leg under my butt to keep myself upright.

"How's work going? I heard some story on the news the other night about a raid you guys had done. Some lab or something," I asked them.

"Oh, yeah, that was my team. We actually left with a lot of evidence which will be good for a new case we're building against The Solution's Chief Lieutenant," said Kane.

"Oohh, interesting. That guy, Sergeant Carmichael, right? He's always given me the creeps. He comes across so robotic on TV when they interview him. What did he do? Assault? Murder?" I asked.

"No, nothing like that. Just some nepotism stuff. It's never as scandalous as people think," Kane answered.

"No, his charges aren't very exciting, but you should see some of this stuff from the raid. Some new state-of-the-art ParColm Vials. These ones secretly take DNA samples without anyone knowing. The Solution is growing their database with more details from citizens than was ever agreed upon, and it is a complete human privacy violation. We're going to stop them before this ever happens, of course," Camellia said with more passion than I have ever had for anything in my life. "Go get that one scanner we found. It was one of the original models. I wonder if it still works. We should all try it out."

Kane headed down their hallway to the office. Just then, I noticed Milo shifting awkwardly in his chair. At first, I think he must have been as uncomfortable in these chairs as I was, and then he asked where the washrooms were. Camellia directed him down the hall just as Kane came back into the room and handed Camellia a black duffel bag full of what looked like a mixture of medical equipment and electronics.

"Here it is," she said, as she pulled out a narrow grey metal tube with a small digital screen on the side and an electrical plug coming out the end. "Can you believe they used to have to plug these things in. And even then, they shorted out all the time." Camellia plugged the device into the wall. "Who wants to go first? Let's see if this thing still works."

Kane got up and Camellia swiped the wand over the back of his neck. "Hold still," she said, "these older ones are finicky." Kane stood for a long time before a beep finally came out of the device. "There we go, it's starting to register. 18 years 4 days 3 hours. Wow, it worked. I'm kind of shocked. Dahl, your turn."

Camellia scanned mine. Slowly, the screen illuminated with text saying 55 years 3 months 12 days.

"Long live the lucky one," Camellia said, as I rolled my eyes. Then I took the scanner from her hand and scanned her neck. Eventually, the numbers show up. 15 years 11 months 2 days. Camellia and I both looked towards the hall, realising that Milo hadn't re-emerged from the bathroom.

"I'd better go check on him," I said, wondering what could be keeping him.

I knocked on the door lightly. "Milo, it's me. Everything okay?"

"Urggh, I'm not feeling so hot. I think there must have been some avocado in those sushi rolls. I have a pretty bad intolerance to avocado. Sorry."

"Oh, no. I didn't know that. Can I do anything?" I said, feeling really bad for Milo and thinking how uncomfortable he must be.

"I think I should just head home. Do you mind calling me a cab? You can stay and take my car home."

"No, no. I'll drive you. Let me just go say goodbye to Camellia and Kane."

Milo spent the hour-long drive doubled over in the passenger seat. He bolted for the bathroom as soon as we got to his place. I offered to stay and look after him, but he'd insisted I go home. I could tell he was embarrassed about what was to come, so I obliged. He told me he'd call me in the morning.

When the phone rang first thing in the morning, I answered it half asleep without glancing at the name, assuming it was Milo — but it was Camellia.

"Morning," she said with way too much enthusiasm considering the early hour.

"Hey," I said groggily.

"Are you still in bed? I've already run 10k and checked in at the office," Camellia said.

"And that's why you'll leave a legacy on this planet long after you're gone and I'll just leave a huge imprint on my mattress," I said.

"Fair enough. How's Milo doing? I felt so bad you guys had to leave."

"I know. Me, too. I haven't heard from him yet. I'm sure he's fine. He's probably just embarrassed. We had a great time, though. Oh, hang on… I'm just getting a text from him now."

I read it out loud. "'Morning. Sorry about last night. I'm feeling much better. Wanna meet for breakfast?' I'm texting him back an emoji of an avocado and toast."

"Nice," Camellia said. "Well, let's get together again soon. I'm happy for you, Dahl"; and before I could thank her, the line went dead.

✳ ✳ ✳

As we get further and further out of the city and make our way onto the highway, I am thinking about the times we'd met up with Camellia and Kane in the last few months, going on double dates to dinner and a concert once. Everyone always seemed to have a great time. Kane even got Milo tickets to an exclusive art exhibit happening in the city, and the two of them went together.

I am starting to think it is weird that Kane hasn't said anything, but soon realise that Camellia must have told Kane not to mention anything about Milo, at least for now. We all have enough to deal with in the next few days.

We turn off the highway and drive down a one-lane paved road for several miles. It's lined on each side with fields and small farms. There are horses and barns and hay bales. As a kid I couldn't wait to get away from all this open space and monotony, but driving down this familiar road today I can appreciate its beauty and simplicity. We turn right onto a red shale road that leads up a tree-lined hill which opens up to a small paved area for parking in front of a white and green building with a sign that says 'Dobbs' Greenhouse and Nursery', and below a smaller sign that says 'Closed Indefinitely'. The grass surrounding the building is perfectly manicured and there are potted plants lining the pathway and giant hanging baskets full of flowers. Kane drives the car down the road to the left and tucked behind a gathering of spruce trees there is a clearing where a two-storey yellow house sits. The same house where we were born and raised. With its white-framed windows, wraparound porch and view down the hill overlooking the lake, it looks picture-perfect.

Now that we have parked, I can see Violet has started to stir. I know that she'll need to nurse right away and I'd rather not do that with a full audience of people staring at us, so I tell Camellia and Kane to go in ahead. I grab Violet and a blanket out of the car before anyone notices we've arrived and tuck us down out of sight behind a big oak tree. I sit down with my back against the thick trunk and position Violet, who sleepily begins to feed. At her one-month check-up, the doctor was very happy with her progress and she said she had doubled her birth weight; another important milestone Milo would have known all about. I wasn't surprised she'd put on the weight, since she seems to be eating all the time and it is taking about half an hour to nurse her every time. As Violet feeds, I look around the property and notice for the first time how different it looks with all the equipment gone. Usually, there were a handful of tractors and combines parked by the shed. I realise that also missing is my Dad's favourite red Ford truck.

Neither Camellia nor myself would have any need for an old farm truck, but it occurs to me that it's the kind of thing Dad would have wanted to pass down to one of his kids. This would be a Rowan thing, I think, looking over at his tree across the yard. I haven't been letting myself get emotional about Dad yet. I've been emotional enough for the past month worrying about Milo and adjusting to the hormones from a new baby, but seeing the empty parking space for the truck in the yard I find myself starting to sob. Poor Violet is startled by the tears dropping down onto her face and stops nursing. I stand up to sway her and burp her as I continue to sniffle silently. Then, off in the distance is a familiar rumbling sound of a diesel engine coming up the driveway and I can see Dad with his tanned arm out the window, smiling as he pulls into his usual spot in the driveway.

"Hi, kiddo," he says, reaching his arm out around my neck as he pulls me and Violet in. "And hello little miss. Pleasure to meet you." He reaches out his big calloused hand and strokes her face with his pointer finger. I try to wipe away the tear stains from my cheek without him noticing and he pulls me in tighter and says, "None of that now. We can't let your mother see you doing that. We have a full week together. Let's enjoy it." We walk back towards the house and I ask where Mom is.

"Your mother has planned a big BBQ for tomorrow night. I told her to keep it simple, but I think the whole county is coming out, so she has been running around getting everything sorted."

"Is this what you want, Dad?" I ask sceptically, as he starts to carry my suitcase up the steps onto the wrap-around porch.

"Of course not, but it's been a good distraction for your mother, so you know me, go with the flow."

After I have unpacked, and set up my childhood bedroom with all the things Violet and I will need for the next month, I head out to the porch to see my dad sitting on an Adirondack chair with Violet asleep against his chest. He has one hand holding up her bottom and the other one holding a beer. I pause before I open the screen door and commit this scene to memory. This will be my father's only week as a grandparent, and he already looks like it's a job he was born to do.

Camellia and Kane have headed out for a walk, and I sit down next to my dad, both of us looking out over the field and lake below, and I catch him up on what I've been working on and what life with Violet has been like. He tells me more about the sale of the greenhouse and the details of the estate. I can tell there is something he's wanting to say and I just blurt it out to get rid of the awkward air.

"You're wondering about Milo, right, Dad?" He drinks down the last swallow of his beer and runs his hand over the top of his grand-daughter's hair and then stares me straight in the eyes.

"I haven't asked for much for this week. I didn't want a service or a lot of fuss. I just wanted our family together. Now, I've asked your mother not to mention that man or ask you about what happened. All that matters to me is that you are home and I got to meet my grand-daughter. I want you to try and get along with your mother this week, and more importantly, after this week. Do you understand? She's going to need you, and I bet you're going to need her, too."

I nod my head and give dad's hand a squeeze. We both look down below at the highway and see a black SUV turn right up the hill. "Here we go," says Dad with a deep sigh.

Chapter Ten
Milo — DD 0 years, 4 months, 21 days

I tried to stay hidden, and spent days filled with paranoia that the same grey sedan was following me. When I finally felt like I had lost them, I spent a month holed up in a motel feeling sorry for myself and drinking myself into oblivion. Then one night I had a dream about my mom. She was in her usual messed-up state, like she always was towards the end of her life. I couldn't understand what she was saying, but she was violently throwing books at me. One after another, as I was hiding under the kitchen table, covering my face. When she finally stopped and I opened my eyes, I saw all my childhood books lying around me in pieces on the floor. I woke up in a sweat with a massive hangover. I leaned over to the nightstand beside me and turned on the light. I sat up in bed and thought about those books for the first time. I remembered the last time I had looked at them was the day mom died and I was visited by the people from The Solution and Dr Malcolm. Being the co-creator of the ParColm Vial and one of the men behind The Solution, I never understood why he gave me his business card that day, but he told me to call him if I ever needed anything. I had never wanted anything from that man since mom had always been fearful of anything to do with that organisation. But, as I lay cold and shivering in my filthy motel room, alone and depressed, I decided I had nothing to lose. That was my rock-bottom. That's when I decided I would fight for my life. Dr Malcolm had given me a card that day with his information on how to contact him. So, I had one connection out there who might be able to help me. It was worth a try. And if it failed, I'd be dead anyway.

Chapter Eleven
Dahlia — DD 64 years, 5 months, 20 days

Twelve years after Rowan's death, my Grandpa was the next person to die in our family. I was in the tenth grade and remember it being as normal a passing as could be expected. By this point, Mom had been on medication for several years to help stabilise her moods, and thanks to her therapist, Dr Melman, Rowan's coffin hadn't been dug up again. But she hadn't had to face another death yet, and since her father didn't believe in finding out his Death Date, this one came as a surprise.

My grandpa was born and raised at the farm and had brought up his own family there, making a modest living as a barley farmer. After my parents had married and returned from college in the city, my grandpa was ready to slow down, so they moved in and took over the farm. Grandpa settled into an assisted living facility and while his mind was still sharp as a tack, his body couldn't keep up. Mom still saw him a few times a week and always had my dad go pick him up and bring him for Sunday dinners at the farm. It was the only meal of the week where we pretended to pray, for Grandpa's sake. After dinner, Dad would take Grandpa out in his truck for a drive around the perimeter of the farm, before taking him back to his home. He always liked to see the different fields and how the crops were doing. Once a farmer, always a farmer. He had no shortage of ideas and opinions on what my dad should do to improve things. Dad should have had holes right through his tongue from how hard he had to bite it on those drives.

At the end of the drive, on a crisp fall day in October, Dad parked the truck in the usual spot and jumped out to offer grandpa a hand getting out. Of course, a proud man, he swore under his breath and brushed my dad's arm away. "I can get out of a damn truck. I'm not useless yet," he said, as Dad backed away and started up the pathway towards the house, shaking his head at his stubborn father-in-law. As Dad rounded up the steps towards the porch, he looked back to see my grandpa collapsed on the ground beside the truck. Dad raced back down towards him, but knew instantly that he had died. Dad panicked because he had no idea how Mom would handle the death of her dad, especially just outside our house. He lifted my grandpa back into the truck and drove him back into town. When he got to the seniors' home, he told the nurse at the desk that grandpa had died on the drive. The Solution authorities were notified and dad came home and told mom. He left her in her room and came to tell me, as I was doing my homework at the kitchen table; then he picked up the phone and called Camellia, who had moved into the city the year before and was in her first year of college, studying political sciences. Camellia told Dad that she would talk to her professors the next day and get home as soon as she could. I was so relieved to know she'd be home soon and Dad and us two girls could hunker down and weather the storm of Mom together. But much to everyone's surprise, Mom emerged from her room the next morning looking rested and stoic. She asked Dad and me if we felt like waffles for breakfast and went down to the basement to fetch the barely used waffle iron. I shot Dad a confused look and he said, "Just go with it" with a sigh. By the time Camellia arrived home later that afternoon, Mom had been into town to clear out Grandpa's room at the home and visited the cemetery and funeral home.

"Surely by tonight she's going to have a meltdown, right?" Camellia said to me. But she didn't. She had moments of sadness, where she would cry when talking about Grandpa, when people visited to pay their respects, or while she made the funeral arrangements, but she was handling this death so normally we couldn't believe it. If anything, it gave her a new lease on life. But part of that included her taking an extra interest in me. She would tell me I spend too much time in my room on my computer, that when my sister was in high school, she was part of the debate club, on the volleyball team and was valedictorian. She had so many friends and I was just locked away in my room all day. But the real guilt-inducer she flung at me, something I knew we all thought, but never said aloud, was that I had the most amount of time left to live of any of us, so I should be making the most of my life.

I tried to get Dad to get her off my back, but he said to give it some time. She just needed something to focus on while she grieved and that it would all pass. At least he thought so. None of us really knew what to do with Mom when she was 'grieving', so I let her make me her new pet project. Just to get her to lay off, I signed up for the yearbook committee. I figured I could at least work on the digital layout with my skillset, and it would be good to add to my college applications in a few years. And in the end, it wasn't a total waste of time. I met a cute boy who was a budding photographer, named Camden.

After a week of Mom's new hobbies, which included Yoga and green smoothies, we were all getting ready to head down to the cemetery for the service. Mom came out of her room in a stunning blue floral dress that matched her eyes. When my Dad asked if she might want to wear something a little more subdued, Mom said something about only having one life to live, so why do it in black? Camellia and I rolled our eyes at each other as we had been doing all week.

A small group of people from Grandpa's seniors' home, long-time neighbours and friends gathered at the graveside. Mom greeted them all warmly as if this was a birthday party we were all attending, and not a funeral. By the time the ceremony was to commence, Camellia, Dad, and I stood near the grave, waiting for Mom to join us. As she made her way to the front, she let out a guttural shriek. The crowd fell silent as we all looked over at Mom. "This is the wrong spot! He's not supposed to be here!" Mom was screaming at the funeral director, and Dad was trying to calm her down.

"I know it's hard to believe he's gone, honey. But he's at peace. It's okay," my dad was trying to reassure Mom, who it seemed had just now realised her dad had died.

"No, that's not it. Look, he's supposed to be buried here next to Mom, his wife, not two plots over."

Everyone's eyes fell to the ground as we read the headstones, and sure enough she was right. There had been a mix-up, and in the plot where Grandpa was meant to be buried, someone else had been occupying it for what appeared to be several years. Unable to pull herself together, my mother refused to go on with 'this charade' of a service and waited in the back of the hearse alone. Mom's outburst had changed the tone of the gathering, so no one really knew what to do next. Finally, one of Grandpa's friends piped up and shared a quick fishing story that made everyone laugh, a nurse from his home spoke about how kind he had been and even Dad made a small speech about the head-strong but big-hearted man he'd had as a father-in-law. It was not quite the memorial any of us were expecting, but we honoured Grandpa the best we could under the circumstances. We all met Mom back in the hearse and drove home in silence, other than the sound of Mom's muffled sobs.

When Mom slept through the next morning's Yoga class, and the kale in the fridge for her smoothies went mouldy, we knew that this 'new lease on life' phase of hers was over. She threw herself back into the greenhouse and left me alone again. Camellia went back to school, and Dad was able to have everything sorted out with Grandpa's grave, though I doubt if Mom has ever visited Grandpa or Grandma there again.

Chapter Twelve
Dahlia — DD in 54 years, 7 months, 21 days

After a marathon family dinner and evening catch-up, I say goodnight and head to my bedroom for the night. As I feed Violet, propped up on my bed in the room that has remained a time capsule of my childhood, I look around at all the pictures and posters from the past. My graduation photo is sitting on the dresser with a baby photo of me stuck in the corner of the frame. I look down at Violet's face and see if I can find any resemblance. Her features are much darker than mine, with thick dark eyes, eyelashes and brows. All Milo's. The small amount of hair she does have seems wavy and brown, also her dad's. I've always hated my mousy-brown stick-straight hair, and am happy I didn't pass that on. While the top half of Violet's face is Milo's, I think I can see my nose and mouth a little in hers. I hope she gets my height and build, too. While I've never been what anyone would consider athletic, I've always been naturally slim and strong, which I appreciate.

I feed Violet one more time and lay her down in her bassinet. I turn off the light and toss and turn for what feels like forever. Even though I'm exhausted from the drive, the socialising, and the heaviness of this week, somehow, I still can't seem to sleep. In the moonlight my eye catches my bag open on a chair and the book Miguel gave me is sitting on top. I pick it up and turn on the lamp beside me, curious about what kind of novel Miguel would be interested in. *Love in the Time of Cholera* by Gabriel Garcia Marquez. I turn to the first page and am stunned to see familiar handwriting. It is not addressed to anyone and there is no signature, but I know without a doubt who made the inscription.

Keep your heart open to me.

I am getting close to the truth.

I love you both

I am shocked. Does this mean Milo has been in touch with Miguel? He must have seen him if he gave him this book. When? How could Miguel not have told me? I can feel my heart pounding as I reach for my phone to call Miguel, not even thinking about the time it is. As I reach over for my cell phone, a Post-It-Note falls out from inside the book.

You have questions. My dear, I do not have the answers. Just a name: Libby Paris.

Love Miguel

My mind is going a thousand miles a minute. I am so confused. A name. Whose name? Why would he have a name? I don't need a name — I need my boyfriend, the father of my child, who is going to be dead in a few months, to come back to us. I creep out of bed, trying not to wake Violet, and grab my laptop. I start typing in Libby Paris. Paris? That's Milo's last name. Libby. It sounds so familiar. Is that Milo's mother's name? He was always so vague about his family, and especially his relationship with his mom. I just know that she died when he was a teenager. As I type in different variations of the name, I'm racking my brain trying to remember what details Milo shared. Then I remember a couple of days after our first visit at Camellia's house, I had finally got up the nerve to have the dreaded family discussion. We were sitting out on my porch in the evening when I asked Milo to tell me more about his mom.

"She was a wannabe writer. She met my dad at college. He was her professor. He'd published a few things and she thought he was a genius and fell head over heels for him. I think she became his muse or something like that. The problem was he was older, married and already had a family. I guess to my mom that wasn't a deal-breaker. She didn't have a great relationship with my grandpa. He was a workaholic doctor or something. I never met the guy, but he didn't approve of her pursuing a career as a writer, and he was beside himself when he found out she was having an affair with a married professor. I think she cut off all communication with her dad then, but I know she kept cashing the cheques that came her way from him. Let's just say we never went without. She lived a pretty comfortable life for someone who never sold a single word she wrote. From what I remember, it was just me and my mom and every once in a while, the professor would come play house for a little bit and then I wouldn't see him for weeks or months at a time. Then, when I was about seven, everything ended abruptly. We moved towns and I never did see my dad again. I looked him up years ago and he had already died. No mention in his obituary of another family, so I guess the asshole got away with it in the end."

"Why did you move?" I asked, surprised to learn any details about Milo's guarded childhood.

"I never really found out why. I always thought it was because my mom came to her senses, but I was just happy I didn't have to see my dad any more. He was always so awkward with me; even as a kid I could tell he didn't want me. I got in the way of his relationship with my mom. The move was great at first. My mom got a job at the library and we were really happy for a few years; but then she started drinking. She had always suffered from really bad migraines. They started when she was in college, and when they got really bad, drinking was the only thing that seemed to make her feel better. And then, eventually, drinking led to pills and she just spiralled. She overdosed when I was seventeen. I'm sure Maria told you that."

"She told me she had died, yes. But not how," I said, as I held Milo's hand. "That's so awful. I'm so sorry."

"It was really rough. I still managed to graduate somehow, and already had that big scholarship to arts college, but I don't think I properly grieved, and so everything kind of came crashing down while I was away at school. I ended up quitting and didn't touch my art for a couple of years. I got weird jobs and moved around a lot. I finally came back for Oscar's funeral seven years ago, and being back here felt right. It was Miguel who convinced me to give it another go with my art, and everything kind of fell into place after that."

"And now you're a world-famous artist!" I said.

"Yeah, something like that. My pieces tend to be pretty dark and moody. That's my form of therapy, I guess. I need to get that out somewhere or else it would consume me."

***

My search Online for the name Libby Paris turns up nothing that seems to fit the right dates and places that would be a relation to Milo. If she died years ago, how could she help me to find Milo now? I don't know how long I am at it, but eventually I fall asleep. I wake up to Violet's cry, and realise it's morning. Last night felt like a bad dream and I would have thought it was if it weren't for Miguel's note sitting on the nightstand beside me. I can hear the hustle and bustle outside my door, of chairs being rearranged and breakfast being made, so I feed Violet and get us both up and ready for the day. I have to focus on my dad today, and this celebration my mom is throwing for him tonight. Milo's secret plea and Miguel's cryptic name will have to wait.

Chapter Thirteen
Dahlia — DD in 54 years, 7 months, 20 days

It is a beautiful crisp spring day. The smell of vanilla is coming off the yellow flowers blooming on the Wolf Willow trees in the garden. There had been a heavy thunderstorm throughout the night and we'd all spent the morning drying off the lawn furniture and chairs we'd set up that had been soaked overnight. Now early afternoon, with Violet asleep in my arms, my mind keeps flickering back to Miguel and Milo, but I am trying to stay in the moment as people have started to arrive for dad's celebration. From my chair I can see some of dad's old law-firm colleagues, his golf-club buddies, mom's friends from town and even the mayor and his wife. When you live in the same place for as long as they have and run a local business, you get to know just about everyone. My parents have always been very well liked, and the issues we'd experienced growing up with mom's outbursts were kept within the family. From the outside we were the picture-perfect family, and here was the whole town coming together to pay their respects to its patriarch.

I can see my parents greeting everyone out on the grass. My mom is dressed impeccably in a black-and-white-patterned dress with capped sleeves and her hair is curled perfectly with not a piece out of place. My dad has at least shaved, but he's in his classic Hawaiian shirt and tan cargo pants. He has never been one to fuss too much with his appearance, and my mom gave up trying to change that years ago. Of course, he would be dressed like an ironic cruise passenger on a day like today. That's just so dad it makes me smile. Violet starts to wake up and I figure it's time we make our entrance. I look down at my dress and can still see a faint red wine stain that never did come out after last summer. I felt that wearing this yellow sundress would give me courage today since it was lucky for me once before, but somehow now that I'm wearing it, it just reminds me of the man I've lost and the one I'm about to. I get up to go inside to see if I'd packed anything I can change into at the last minute, but before I get the chance, I hear Camellia calling my name from the grass.

"There she is! Dahlia, come down here and say hi to Mrs Goldman." I can see Camellia is standing talking to our old school principal, and from the look on her face she's been stuck in this conversation for a lot longer than she would have liked and is needing some rescuing. I walk towards them with Violet propped up against my shoulder.

"Hello, Dahlia. How nice to see you. I'm sorry it's under such sad circumstances."

"Hi, Mrs Goldman. Thank you for coming today. I'm sure it means a lot to my parents."

"Your family has always been such a big part of the community. Your mother and I play in the same bunco group every month, so she fills me in on what you girls are up to. She's always talking about Camellia's big career with The Cause, and I believe she's mentioned you do something with computers, is that right, Dahlia?"

Before I start to answer and explain what it is exactly I do with computers, Mrs Goldman interrupts me. "Well, and now you are a mother. Isn't that so delightful. I didn't realise you had married," she says.

"Nope, not married. Just me and the baby at the moment. I'm single and ready to mingle, so if you have anyone at the party in mind…," I say with as much sarcasm as possible, much to the horror of Mrs Goldman and the amusement of Camellia.

Most of the afternoon continues with similar conversations. Camellia and I decide we are better off sticking together and navigate the party as a pair so we can save one another from the tough questions like: why don't you come home more often, where is your daughter's father, and the real doozy — will you be moving back to help your mother now? Thank goodness for Violet today, who has been the most amazing prop that conveniently needed changing or would get fussy just when things got extra awkward.

I had just put Violet down for her late-afternoon nap when I came back outside and surveyed the group of about one hundred people. It looked like many had started to dip into the wine we'd put out and it was a fairly upbeat group, considering the purpose of the gathering. My mom was being fussed over by her group of ladies and she looked like she'd been crying on and off for most of the afternoon. I'd heard people retelling old stories of dad to her all day, which kept setting her off. I look around at the groups of men sitting together, between the neighbouring farmers and the town acquaintances, but I can't find dad in the group. As I walk back up towards the house, I notice his red truck is gone. Surely, if there had been a last-minute errand to run, someone other than the guest of honour at his own wake could have done it. The rain from earlier has left tyre tracks heading towards the back forty acres and not towards town. I pop my head inside the old wooden shed beside the greenhouse and sure enough, as expected, there is my old purple bike leaning up against the wall. I wipe off the cobwebs and dust and head off down the dirt lane that leads around the back and down the ravine. At the top of the hill, before it slopes down into a tree-covered marsh, I spot the truck parked down by the slough. It takes me a few minutes to pedal down the hill on a narrow path of trampled hay that's been worn down by tyre tracks. Dad has backed up his truck towards the water and is sitting with the tailgate down, legs dangling over the end, beer in hand.

"You found me," he says, opening up a can of beer for me and patting down a spot beside him, inviting me up into the truck.

"What are you doing down here, Dad?" I say. After spending my entire life on this property, I can count on one hand the number of times I've been down to this spot. Camellia dragged me down here one time as kids in a game of hide and seek gone terribly wrong. We both came back with dozens of mosquito bites and I had a leech stuck to my ankle. My mom was furious when she heard where we'd been and told us we were never allowed down there again.

"I've always liked it down here. It's quiet and secluded, and I can hide out and do my best thinking here. You know, life is all about moments, Dahlia. You have to try your best to move past the bad ones and cherish the good. That's the only real thing I've learned in this life of mine: hang on to your moments," Dad says longingly.

I fight my inner sarcasm to leave *this* moment hanging in the air. I can tell Dad wants to tell me more, maybe reflect on his life, and as uncomfortable as I am with hearing it, and scared about losing the thin hold I have on my emotions, I sit quietly and listen.

"Your mom and I used to come down here when we were first dating. We could hide out in the bushes, if you know what I mean." My dad winks at me as I make the obligatory face all children must make at that thought of their parents, regardless of their age. "Your catholic grandpa kept a very close eye on us around the house, but we'd take the horses out for a ride and could sneak away down here for a little while without raising too many eyebrows. Did you know I proposed to your mom over there?" he says, pointing the top of his beer over to a small clearing in the bushes surrounded by wild flowers. "We would still sneak off down here when you kids were little, after you'd gone to sleep. It was our little romantic place," Dad says, pausing and taking a deep breath on a sweet memory.

It really is a beautiful spot, I think to myself. "No, I didn't know that, Dad. It's a shame this section had to be sold off with the auction. I didn't realise it meant so much to you. But I never remember mom coming down here. She always got mad at us if we ever played on the back half of the land."

"No, honey. Your mother won't miss this place," Dad says, looking down at the murky water below our feet. "This is where you had your accident all those years ago. Your mother only associates this place with bad memories now."

I look up at my dad, surprised to hear an alternate detail to a story I'd heard a thousand times. "My accident happened at the lake. You mean when I was three and almost drowned? That accident?"

"Yes, that one. No, you were down here with me that day. I wanted to build a little dock and had visions of canoeing around this pond. It was a lot deeper back then, before we filled it in. I was taking some measurements and thought you were right behind me when I was getting my tools out of the truck. The next thing I know, I see a pink shirt floating in the water." My dad takes his glasses off and wipes away the water that has started to pool at the sides of his eyes with the telling of a very painful memory. Both my parents had told this story over the years, but with so few details I just assumed I had wandered off at the lake with the family and they grabbed me out of the water. We had always used the word "accident" to describe the event, but from what I'd been told I was no worse for wear when they pulled me out of the water, and after that we were all enrolled in years of swimming lessons and that was that. But that was a fabricated version of the story, apparently.

"I jumped into the water and pulled you out. You couldn't have been under for more than a couple of minutes, but you weren't breathing. I started to do chest compressions and mouth-to-mouth, and thank god it only took a couple of tries and you started to cough. By the time I got you back up to the house, your colour had returned and you were singing your ABCs. I'd never heard such a sweet sound in all my life. We called the doctor in from town to come and check on you and your mother made sure to tell him we didn't want to know your Death Date when he scanned your vial, but that was the breaking point for me. I'd made a promise to your grandfather and your mother when we married that while I wouldn't be practising their religion, I would respect their faith and not find out any of my children's DDs or your mother's. But that was before I saw your life flash before my eyes. I thought I was going to lose you in those minutes after I pulled you out of that water and I had to know how much time I would have left with each one of you. Your mother was furious with me, but I told the doctor to scan each one of you right then. Your mother was trying to hold all of you away from the doctor. It was chaos, and there was so much screaming and cursing. The doctor wasn't sure what to do. Finally, your mother fell to the ground and gave in. She was sobbing into her hands when we found out each one of your fates. Camellia at eight years old had thirty-eight years left; you at three had seventy-seven; and Rowan at twenty-one months old just had three months to live," Dad says, as if he has to heave the words out of his mouth like they were heavy rocks skipping across the pond and sinking deep below the surface.

"Your mother was never quite the same after that day. Something unhinged, and she has always stayed that way. I had the pond filled in, although it's a natural gully, so after it rains like last night, it fills back up for a little while and then drains away. I like to come down here on days like this after the rain and remember our life back then. I still think it's better to know than to live in ignorance, so I don't regret finding out the Death

Dates; but I like to remember the happiest moments in my life before that day, when I wanted to build a dock for a canoe and I had three healthy, happy children and a wife I could sneak around in the bushes with."

Chapter Fourteen
Dahlia — DD in 54 years, 7 months, 18 days

The morning of Dad's Death Day starts like any of the others of the week I've been home. We all have breakfast together and then Dad goes down to the lake to take out his sailboat for one last ride. Kane had gone back to the city a couple of days ago to let us have some family time, and Camellia and I are cleaning up in the kitchen. Both Mom and Violet have gone down for naps. After Dad's party two days ago, Mom had started sleeping a lot and we had suspected she was taking something prescribed by her old doctor to help her through this tough time. Camellia and I have had our concerns about her being so medicated, but know the alternative with her history is probably a much worse scenario. I just hope her prescription has enough refills for the days and weeks to come.

I have just finished up the dishes when the doorbell rings and Camellia goes to answer it. I suspect it is another bouquet of flowers. The town florist must have been especially busy this week since we are getting several deliveries a day. I guess people don't know what to say or do, but to me it seems insensitive to send flowers to an ex-greenhouse owner forced to shut down their business because their husband is dying.

I turn off the tap and can hear Camellia talking to a man at the door.

"He's actually not home right now. He'll be back in about half an hour if you'd like to come in and wait for him, Camden."

I freeze. Camden? Camden Conrad! What is he doing here? I don't have the emotional capacity to deal with this today.

"Thanks, Camellia, but I don't want to disturb your family. I will just wait out on the porch for him. My condolences."

Camellia comes back into the kitchen, pointing over her shoulder and whispering to me. "That was Camden at the door! He's out on the deck," she says with wide eyes.

"Yeah, I heard that. What is he doing here?" I say, flabbergasted.

"I guess he's head of the county's Solution. He said he tried to send someone else, but everyone was tied up. He knew it would be uncomfortable for you. He just needs to check in with Dad and scan his ParColm Vial. He said Dad is registered in some voluntary research initiative or something. I'm going to have to look into this at work. It seems unethical and probably breaches many codes." Camellia pulls out her phone and begins typing away. Her concern for my awkward situation gets trumped by her dedication to her work.

"Oh, god. What are the odds? I think I heard Camden started working for them, but I haven't even thought of him at all since I've been home. And now he's just waiting out there! Should I bring him some coffee or something? This is so unbelievable!" I say.

"I guess. I don't know. Have you been in touch at all after you broke his heart and deserted him?" Camellia says matter-of-factly, barely glancing up from her phone.

"Thanks!" I say, rolling my eyes. "No, not at all. I felt bad at first, but as soon as I got to the city I never did look back. I'm awful. I should go say hi." I take a deep sigh and pour two cups of coffee. "Listen for Violet if she wakes up, please. I really don't want to have *that* conversation, too."

Out on the porch, leaning up against the railing, is the high school boyfriend I left behind eight years ago, although his 6ft 6in frame is hardly recognisable now that he's filled out with muscle and maturity. His hair is shorter and his face looks fuller, but his eyes still smile before his mouth, and thankfully they smile when he sees me.

"Dahlia. Hi! Sorry, I didn't want to disturb you today of all days," he says, looking sheepish. For a split second I see a familiar look in his eyes of the shy sweet boy I used to know who used to hide behind his camera; but in a flash it is gone and left standing in his uniform is someone who now clearly commands a great deal of respect and authority.

"It's okay. It's nice to see you. I brought you some coffee," I say, as I hand him a cup and gesture for him to take a seat beside me. "Dad should be back soon."

"When your Dad's name came up on our database a couple of months ago, I had kind of forgotten he was a Vixit Vitam. Like my parents. They were a lot younger, though," he says, as he looks off down at the lake.

"Oh, ya. Right. I'm sorry." I pause uncomfortably, hoping to change the subject. "How have you been?" I ask.

"Pretty good. I'm a Director with The Solution now. So I handle all the deaths in the county. I don't normally do the house-calls, but there was a staffing issue this week…" He trails off. I can tell he is nervous and rambling.

"A Director. Wow, that's impressive!" I say, trying to seem interested.

"Well, it's a lot more paperwork these days than law enforcement. We still get the odd person trying to tamper with their ParColm Vial and there are always protests, but most of my job is done electronically. We have a huge state-of-the-art database that keeps tabs on everyone so we can get ahead of the deaths instead of waiting until after. I'm the lead agent on a research project that your dad signed up for. It would revolutionise this process."

Before Camden can explain any more, Dad's red truck starts coming up the drive. He smiles at us as he walks up the steps to the porch. "Well, that's a sight I haven't seen in a long time. I used to catch you two kids out here long after curfew. Camden, nice to see you," my Dad says, as he reaches out his hand. I can see the red in Camden's cheeks as he shakes my Dad's hand and stands up straight, returning to business mode.

"Hello, Mr Dobbs." Camden clears his throat as if he's going to launch into a well-rehearsed speech, but Dad cuts him off.

"Yes, I know, I'm sorry. I was supposed to check in at The Solution office this week and have my scan. I have just been enjoying my family and I knew you guys would come find me," My Dad says with a wink. I don't know how he can remain so jovial in his last hours.

"I understand, sir. This will just take a minute." Camden reaches down towards his briefcase.

"I'll leave you guys to it," I say, feeling the tears coming and not wanting to be emotional in front of my ex-boyfriend. "Camden, it was nice to see you. Take care," I say, as I rush inside just as the tears start falling down my face. I go into my room quietly not to wake sleeping Violet and cry soundlessly into my pillow.

***

We spend the rest of the day and evening all huddled together as a family. Subconsciously, we go from room to room as a foursome, trying to squeeze out the last hours we all have together. We all help out in the kitchen, making dinner like a synchronised swimming team moving gracefully around each other, not wanting to create a single ripple in the water. Mom has offered to make Dad his favourite meal for dinner, but he refuses, saying, "That's ridiculous! I'm not on Death Row. I haven't murdered anyone. We have so much food left over from the party. We'll just have some of that."

I notice after the meal that Dad hasn't really eaten much, but he has filled his wine glass up three times. So have I. After we have cleaned up, we all go and sit in the living room, again ridiculously close to one another, as if somehow our closeness will keep Dad alive. The only time anyone leaves the room is if our emotions get the better of us and we excuse ourselves briefly to compose ourselves. It happens a lot. Dad has been adamant about everyone trying to keep it together and we do pretty well, considering. After a few hours of watching some forgettable movie we all glaze over, and Dad says it's time for bed. Saying goodnight and goodbye are too excruciating to handle. Mom has taken a sedative that her doctor prescribed and is already in her bedroom, and I am wondering if I should take something, too. Then I think of Violet and the side effects that could have on my milk and realise I'll have to feel every single painful emotion as the night goes on. Dad pulls both Camellia and me in for a huddle hug like he used to when we were kids. Our heads are all touching and the tears are pooling on the floor below us.

"You girls take care of each other and your mother. I know it won't be easy, but I'm counting on you. You have been the joys of my life. I couldn't be prouder of the women you have become if I had a hundred more years to live to see it." Dad kisses us both on the foreheads.

"I love you, Dad," Camellia says, giving him a tight hug and wiping her face with a Kleenex. "You have been the very best Dad in the world." She backs away and starts to stoically walk off to her room.

"Daddy. No, I'm not ready. No! This isn't fair!" I am hanging off him now, pulling at him to stay with us longer, not to go into his room, where he'll shut the door and we'll never see him again. Camellia turns around and grabs hold of me.

"Dahlia. Enough. Don't make this harder than it needs to be. This is how Dad wants it. We have to respect that. Come on." Camellia holds me by the shoulders and I break free of her and run towards Dad and hug him one last time. I squeeze so tightly I think my arms will fall off.

"I love you, kiddo," he whispers, as he turns towards his door and shuts it behind him.

"Daddddy! Nooooooo!" I sob, falling to the ground. Camellia comes to help me up and we stumble together to my room.

"How about I stay with you tonight? Like we used to when we were little," Camellia says, as we sit down on my bed.

"Yeah, okay. But I don't know how I'm going to get any sleep," I say through my sniffles.

"This should help." Camellia pulls out a giant bottle of Jameson Irish Whiskey. She passes it to me and I take a huge swig and immediately cough and gag as silently as possible not to wake a sleeping Violet. We pass the bottle back and forth in the dark until we lay down with our heads touching on the one pillow.

"I don't know how you can be so rational all the time. All I can think about is Dad lying in there, breathing in and out, until click, he won't be. It makes me want to scream and vomit at the same time," I say.

"I know. I do, too, but this is how it is. I think it would be worse if we didn't know. We've had all this time to prepare and we got to say a proper goodbye. It's kind of beautiful to go out the way you want, isn't it?"

"I guess so. I'm just grateful I don't have to do this alone. I know for sure I wouldn't be able to handle Mom alone. What do you think she's going to be like tomorrow?"

"I don't know. But we'll figure it out together," Camellia says, as she yawns.

***

My head is pounding and my mouth is so dry. I open one eye and scan around the room. There is a tiny sliver of light coming through the blinds, and I can just make out Violet asleep in her bassinet. I look over at the clock and see it's 6.45am. That is the longest stretch Violet has slept in a row. Good girl, I think to myself, smiling, and then I roll over and see Camellia asleep beside me and I instantly remember last night and why we are together in bed. Dad! I let out a moan and tears start to fall again. I am paralysed, unable to move, wondering what needs to be done now. I lay back down, thinking that Camellia is definitely the better one to handle the situation. I'll wait for her to wake up. Then I feel a heavy stretching pain in my chest and realise I need to nurse. I'm so uncomfortably full of milk but can't possibly feed Violet after all I drank last night. I sneak out of the bed and creep open the door. I walk out into the palely lit hallway I've walked down a thousand times before, but strangely it feels different. It's like the air has changed. Somehow it feels staler now. I make my way to the kitchen and rummage around my bag of Violet's things. I find my breast pump and attach it to my bra. I instantly feel relief. I also find an Advil in the cupboard and tilt my head under the tap and feel chills all over my body as the cold water splashes my face and coats my sore, dry throat. I wipe my mouth with the back of my pyjama sleeve and open the fridge to find a bottle for Violet. She'll be waking up any minute, I'm sure. As I heat up the bottle, I look out of the window and see a dark caravan pulling up the driveway. Who could that be at this time of the morning? Then it hits me. The coroner! Oh my gosh. It's happening now? Is this normal? What do I do? I run down the hall into my room and yell at Camellia.

"Wake up! The coroner is here. Did you know they'd be here this early?"

Camellia rolls over and rubs her eyes and sits up, shaking her head from side to side as if she is slowly processing the information. "Coroner? What…? Oh god. Dad. Okay. What time is it?" she says groggily.

"Almost seven." My voice is still loud and it startles Violet. She starts to cry and I pick her up and try to balance her on my lap and feed her a bottle while still pumping the wasted milk. Camellia is throwing on last night's clothes and rushing out of the room. "Come on!" she yells after me. "We have to deal with this now!"

I throw a thin crochet blanket over the top of the front of myself, making sure not to cover up Violet's face, and follow Camellia out towards the front door. Before anyone has a chance to ring the door bell, Camellia has opened the screen and invited the three men in Solution uniforms into our home.

"Camellia Dobbs-Montgomery," she says, always the professional. "This is my sister Dahlia, and niece Violet." She looks over at my dishevelled self and apologises. "I'm sorry, we weren't expecting you quite so early."

"Good morning, ma'am." The tall, balding man in front nods his head to Camellia and reaches out his hand. "I'm Sergeant McLean, this is Deputy Smythe and Doctor Bowden," he says assertively, pointing at the two men standing behind him. "Yes. It is rather unusual for us to be conducting our business at this time…"

Before Sergeant McLean has a chance to continue, Camellia has cut him off.

"Doesn't the family of the deceased have twelve hours post-mortem with the body?" Camellia says, raising her voice slightly.

"Yes, ma'am. Typically, that is the allotted time; however, under these circumstances we have to act rather quickly. Could you please show us to the body now?"

"No, I'm sorry I can't. What do you mean 'these circumstances'? We haven't had our proper time to say goodbye. We have a right to that." She is now shouting.

"Of course you do. However, I'm afraid your father has waived that right. We will conduct our business as quickly as possible and be out of your way as soon as we can."

"The hell you will!" Camellia yells, as her body starts to shake.

"Girls? What's going on? Who are these men? Your father…" We all look down the hall towards Mom, who is emerging from her room in her bathrobe. She looks as horrible as we all feel.

"Mom, it's okay. Don't worry," I say, gesturing for Mom to join us in the living room. I turn towards Camellia, pleading with my eyes that she doesn't escalate this further, scared of what reaction Mom will have. "Camellia. Calm down. These men are just doing their job. It's okay." Before she starts up again, I interject and move between her and our guests. "I understand you have to do what you have to do. But we were not expecting this and aren't quite prepared. Could you please just give us one minute of privacy and then you can go ahead."

"Of course. If you'd like to take a look at the case file, all the documentation should be in order. Please don't take too long. Time is of the essence." The men head out to the porch and I take Mom's hand.

"Morning, Mom. It's okay. These men are just here to take care of Dad. Why don't you sit down here and finish feeding Violet?" I help Mom down to the couch and pass Violet to her. I can see the colour come back to her face as she focuses on her grand-daughter. Violet smiles sweetly up at the familiar face of her grandma. "Okay, Camellia, do you want to look this over? I mean, this is more your wheelhouse, but I kind of think everything is legit. The study, I mean…" Just as I hand over the folder to Camellia, the shorter man, Deputy something or other, comes back in through the sliding glass porch doors.

"Excuse us again. I'm afraid we have run out of time to have the trial assessment done back at our headquarters. We must remove the ParColm Vials no less than four hours after discharge, and in the case of Mr Dobbs, we are coming up on that end. We have two options: either we take him back to The Solution's HQ in town and follow regulatory post-mortem protocol, but that means he will be exempt from the trial; or we will have to perform the vial removal here."

"Here! Are you fucking insane? There is no way you are doing an autopsy on my father in our home. Get the hell out of here, all of you!" Camellia throws the case file at the deputy as she lunges towards him violently.

"Camellia, calm down! They are just doing their jobs. Come on. Dad volunteered for this study. He would have wanted his information to matter. Remember last night, you were the one who told me we had to respect his wishes. You stay with Mom and Violet. I will help them sort this out."

Camellia reluctantly moves into the living room and sits down next to Mom. I'm both shocked and impressed at my level of calm. How did I become the voice of reason today? I guess everyone reacts differently to grief, and today it's Camellia's turn to feel the big emotions.

The three men follow me down the hallway with a large metal rolling case full of supplies. I can only imagine what they plan to do with them, but I try to banish that from my thoughts. "He's right in here. Let me know if you need anything." I wipe the tears away that I just realise are sliding down my face. I'm not sure when I started crying; it could have been the moment the men came to the door, but I was too distracted by all the chaos.

"You are welcome to come in and say goodbye while we set up," the doctor says kindly.

"No. That's okay. Thank you, though. That's not my Dad in there any more. He's moved on."

***

After what feels like hours, but is really more like forty-five minutes, the three men wheel out a black tarp-covered gurney to their van. Camellia yells after them that she has written down all their names and ID numbers and that their superior will be hearing from her. Her and Mom both take some of Mom's sedatives and go back to bed. I'm restless, but otherwise okay. I decide to burn off some energy and take Violet for a walk around the farm in her baby carrier. It is a bright shiny morning and I walk along the gravel path back behind the crops to the top of the property line. At this high point is the best view down towards the lake, and it is a crystal-clear calm morning with the slightest breeze. "Would have been a great day for sailing," I say out loud. I'm trying out this 'talking to him like he can hear me' thing. I'm not sure it's for me — my cynical side feels kind of silly — but there's another part of me that can feel him somehow. On my way back towards the house, I see Dad's pick-up truck parked right where it always is, and I decide to climb in. Before I can sit down, I spot a white envelope on the driver's seat addressed to me. I climb in and tear open the letter.

127

Dearest Dahlia,

I know I told you I wasn't going to do this, but I had to write you a letter. There are things I just couldn't say in person in the end and I hope you understand. As you know, your mother has made arrangements for me to be buried under the big weeping willow tree beside Rowan's tree. This is comforting to your mother. She needs something tangible she can visit and feel a connection to. After Rowan's death, your mother's sanity was rooted in the earth. It was a special kind of therapy to her, and the mechanics of growing and nurturing her plants kept her going. I quit my job at the law firm which I loved to help her build the business. I saw the pleasure it brought her and I was most happy when she was happy. But now I can't stand the idea of rotting away underground. I want to be cremated. I want to be sprinkled all over these fields where I watched you and your sister grow up. I want to float on the lake where I spent my life sailing. I want to be free. Just like Rowan. I couldn't leave my baby boy in the ground, either. Your mother must never know, but after the first time she dug up his coffin all those years ago something snapped in me, too. I couldn't leave him out there. I had a friend of mine cremate him and we returned the empty coffin back under his tree. I've been spreading Rowan's ashes around for years. It's kept him with me in a way. And you thought your mother was the crazy one! I have already made arrangements and my same friend is going to handle everything, so your mother will never know. She can go out to 'my tree' and talk to me until she's blue in the face, because that is what she needs. What I need is to be set adrift and I need you to do that. Not all at once. You can keep me on your shelf for a while, but when you're ready, let me go.

I also need to tell you that I had a visit from Milo. A couple of days before you came home, he stopped by the house. Your mother wasn't home, thank goodness, and he confided in me his situation. Maybe because he knew I was dying, he trusted me. I want you to know that I trust him. We didn't have long together, but I liked the guy. I know that would matter to you and I'm glad that it does. He's very direct and intense and I could tell how much he loves you. He seems like the kind of guy who would move mountains for you. And I think that's what he's trying to do. You need to find him, Dahlia.

And last, but not least, I want you to take my truck. Don't roll your eyes. I know I should have sold it and I almost did, but I couldn't get rid of the old thing. You take my truck, your little girl and go find Milo.

I am proud of you and love you!
Dad

Chapter Fifteen
Milo — DD 0 years, 4 months, 17 days

Dahlia's dad is dead now. I'm devastated that I'm not there to comfort her. I've known about this date as long as I've known her. She never talked too much about her mom, but she adored her father and told me all sorts of stories about the kind, selfless man who raised her. They had been close, in a way you're supposed to be with your dad, a way I had only imagined in my life. I knew I had to meet the man responsible for raising Dahlia into the woman she is now. The woman of my dreams. The mother of my child. It was a big risk to take to expose myself in that way. I was sure I was being followed again, but it was worth it. And now I'm more resolved than ever to put things right. I gave Dahlia's dad my word, and I won't let him down.

Chapter Sixteen
Dahlia — DD 63 years, 6 months, 13 days

Camden and I had been dating for about six months by the time of my sixteenth birthday. I'd just got my driver's licence and dad was going out of town for a fishing trip with his old lawyer colleagues. He told me I could take his truck to the drive-in on Saturday, as long as I took Camellia with me. Neither of us were thrilled with that idea, but we hatched our own plan where I would drop her off at a house party happening in town and pick her up after the movie. Camden and I had been fooling around the way most teenagers do by this point, but I think both of us were expecting things to go a little farther on this night. After dropping Camellia off, Camden and I parked at the very back row of the drive-in lot. It was the darkest and most deserted back there and I had brought plenty of blankets and pillows to fill up the box of the truck. We watched the first half of the movie quietly, each pretending to concentrate on the plot and waiting for the other one to make a more serious move. When nothing was happening, and I felt like time was running out on our big night, I turned my body away from him in an adolescent pout and laid on my side, creating a big space between us under the blanket.

"What is it? What's wrong?' he asked.

"Nothing. I just thought maybe we'd... I don't know. Never mind."

"Oh. Well, I wasn't sure if you wanted to. We've never really talked about it... and Gus thought you probably wouldn't want to."

"You talked to Gus about this? Oh my god. I can't believe you! That's none of his business." I inched even farther away from him, still lying on my side.

"Well, I'm sure you talked to Marianne!" Camden said.

"Maybe I did. So what? It's different for girls. It's a way bigger deal for us. I just wanted some advice." I was glad I was facing away from him, as my cheeks felt hot as I admitted my nerves.

"Advice for what? Like how?"

"I guess. Or like how it'll feel. Will it hurt? I don't know. Never mind," I said, embarrassed but still sulking.

"No, it's okay. I'm nervous, too. But I love you and we can just take it slow and do whatever feels right." Camden wrapped his long arms around me and pulled me back into his chest. His embrace was always so tight and enveloping, it was a guaranteed cure to calm me down. He started kissing the back of my neck with his hand on my stomach. He slowly started turning me back over to face him and my mouth met his half way. His hand on my stomach moved up under my sweater and he started to feel for the back of my bra. He was clumsy, fidgeting with the clasp until he finally undid it. As soon as that happened, it was like the flood gates opening, and we both frantically started removing clothing under the blanket. He reached under the covers for his jeans pocket and pulled out a condom. I snickered at the package, thinking this was a scene from a movie, and I felt very adult all of a sudden.

After he struggled to open it and moved around under the blanket to put it on, he looked me straight in the eyes and told me he loved me again. "We can stop whenever you want."

"Okay," I said nervously. Camden moved on top of me and I let out a deep exhale from the weight of his body, but also the weight of what was about to happen. As he adjusted himself, I felt a pinch and then pressure. It didn't hurt, but it felt unlike anything I had ever experienced before.

"Is this okay?" he said breathlessly.

"Yeah," I said, reassuring him. "Is it happening?" I asked, unsure of what it should feel like.

"Yes. I think so. Wait, how about now?"

I felt a sharp pain and then motion. The truck was moving underneath me as he thrusted gently on top of me. I dug my nails into his shoulders. Marianne warned me about this. She said the first time you just have to get through it, and after that it would be nice. I found Camden's lips again and felt myself getting slipperier, which made things feel better. I started to move in-sync with his body and lost myself in the sensations that were firing off all over my body. But just like that, I lost my focus and it started to feel tight again. I tried to distract myself and I listened back into the words of the movie. Over Camden's heavy breathing and grunting, I could hear music and yelling. A distant yell that was getting closer and closer.

"Leeeahhh, Meeeelia, Anddd." What was that sound, I thought to myself. It started to get louder and clearer and I realised it wasn't the movie at all. It was someone shouting in the parking lot.

"Camden, do you hear that?" I said, as I moved sharply away, and he jolted up, rolling to the side of the truck. I gathered the blankets around me and looked up over the side of the truck just as I heard the sound more clearly.

"DAHLIA! CAMELLIA! ROWAN! Where are you?" Through the darkness, between vehicles, I could see a figure in white walking barefoot down the dirty field. When the movie screen turned to a bright sunny scene, the white figure appeared visibly to be my mother in a long white pyjama shirt and nothing else.

"DAHLIA! CAMELLIA! ROWAN!" she yelled out again in a daze.

"Shut up. Someone shut her up!" I heard another person yell out of their vehicle's window.

"MOM?! What are you doing? Over here," I screamed, realising I was naked from the waist down. I had gotten her attention and she started to stumble towards the truck. Camden went stark white and we both frantically tried to put back on our clothes. I was able to get myself together first and threw a blanket over the top of a shocked Camden, still half-crouched over his jeans. I hopped up out of the side of the truck and tucked my bra into my back pocket and it started to fall to the ground. I realised quickly that my mother was in no way noticing the compromising scene she almost witnessed. I could tell she was in some kind of trance, as I looked down and saw her feet all covered in mud and blood.

"Mom, did you walk here?" I said in disbelief. It was at least five miles across the highway and through a wooded area.

"Everyone is gone. Everyone. I checked the beds. My girls are gone. And Rowan. Where is his crib? He's not there. His crib is gone. And Daniel. He's gone. He's gone. Everyone is gone." My mom started to sob. It was unclear if she recognised me or was just rambling to anyone that would have listened.

"Mom. Mom. Shhhh! Look at me. I'm right here. I'm here. It's Dahlia. Mom, we're okay. Camellia and I are fine. Daddy… er… Daniel is away this weekend, remember? He went fishing. Rowan's crib…" I hesitated. Years ago, after the greenhouse incidents, Mom's therapist told us that the best way to deal with Rowan questions was by diverting. When she was in a 'state', it didn't help to get her more worked up.

"Let's go get Camellia and we'll help you find Rowan's crib. Okay?"

By now, Camden was standing sheepishly behind me, wide-eyed and bashful. I helped Mom into the back seat of the truck and climbed in beside her. I tossed the keys to Camden as we exchanged glances in the rear-view mirror. I mouthed the words 'I'm sorry' to him and he smiled sweetly and gave me a wink. I felt butterflies in my stomach thinking about what we had just done and excited about when we would get to do it again. I couldn't wait to tell Marianne that it was actually okay for the most part. But first, I'd have to drag Camellia out of her party and we were going to have to call Dad. Mom was going to need to start up therapy again that week, and that was a whole family commitment.

Chapter Seventeen
Dahlia — DD in 54 years, 4 months, 16 days

A couple of days after Dad's death, once his affairs had been put in order, Kane came back to fetch Camellia to head back to the city. Camellia had done her very best to be patient with Mom, because, like me, she'd promised Dad she would, but she had reached her maximum capacity for emotions after forty-eight hours. I, on the other hand, am supposed to stay the month. It had been a difficult week tip-toeing around Mom's delicate state, but also dealing with my own grief. I find staying out of the house and taking Violet on long walks around the farm helps. On my way back from our walk this morning, I am surprised to see the light on in the greenhouse. I look in one of the big front windows to see Mom organising some empty pots. When she sees me in the doorway, she says that she wants to get her plants ready for Lilac Festival in a couple of weeks. I am able to hide my surprise and leave her to it. This seems like a good sign that she is occupying herself with something productive. I will never understand her connection to plants, but I am grateful for it for the first time today.

After reading Dad's letter constantly over the past few days, I am obsessing about the thought that Milo had been to see him. Finally, with Mom busy in the greenhouse, I am able to delve into the box of things I'd taken from Milo's studio last month. With Violet laid out on a blanket beside me, I dump out the contents of the box and start rifling through old books and papers. There are receipts, bank statements and the rental agreement for his studio. Mixed in with a pile of sketch pads is an old leather notebook monogrammed with the initials I.P. on the cover. It looks like a well-used notebook from the scuffed-up cover, but the first half of the pages have been ripped out. The rest of the book is blank and untouched, other than a few loose pages tucked into the back. Out of the book falls a crayon drawing of two stick figures holding hands. It's obviously done by a small child, but the detail is remarkable in their faces; it must have been done by Milo at a very young age, with his talent being clear early on. As I skim my fingers over the pages to see if anything else is tucked inside, I find a folded-up piece of yellowed newspaper. I open it and see it's an article from the local *Advocate* newspaper.

The Grim Reaper Dies

The infamous doctor and creator of the ParColm Vial, Ignacio Parisi, has died at the age of fifty-four. Dr Parisi invented the controversial vial with the help of his protégé Dr Paul Malcolm. Dubbed 'The Grim

Reaper' or 'Dr Evil' by many after the intense backlash and outrage at the immediate implementation of the "death" vials, officially called ParColm Vials, Dr Parisi maintained his invention would "save humanity from itself". Drs Parisi and Malcolm were the first to have vials randomly chosen and implanted in themselves, and ironically, Dr Parisi's vial only had three weeks left until his expiry date. There was a large group of protesters gathered outside of The Core's Solution headquarters, cheering at the death of the doctor. The charismatic Dr Malcolm refused to stop for comment on his partner's passing, saying only, "he was a genius and true friend", as he made his way into the building through the frenzied crowd.

Ignacio Parisi is survived by his adult daughter Isobel Parisi.

Isobel Parisi. I.P. The initials on the front of the notebook. Parisi? Why would Milo have Isobel Parisi's — daughter of Dr Evil — notebook. Isobel Parisi. As I say her name over and over in my head, I finally say it out loud and it catches in my throat as I form the syllables. Pa-ri-si or just Paris. I launch myself off the bed and scramble in my bag to find the book that Miguel gave me. First, Milo's pleading inscription:

Keep your heart open to me.
I am getting close to the truth.
I love you both

And then Miguel's name.

You have questions. My dear, I do not have the answers. Just a name: Libby Paris.

Love Miguel

Libby Paris. With my laptop open beside me, I type into the search bar 'nicknames for Isobel'; and sure enough, number two on the list is exactly what I expected.

- Izzy
- Libby
- Bella

Libby Paris, or Isobel Parisi, which can only mean Milo Paris or Milo Parisi. Milo is the grandson of one of the most reviled men in recent history. The man responsible for so much death and turmoil. Our entire way of being was shifted because of this man. I had never really had any real feelings either way about The Solution of the ParColm Vials. Maybe, because I was going to have a long life, I didn't worry about it too much. I understood something drastic needed to be done and I assumed the people who had come to put this system in place were doing so with everyone's best interests in mind. Even Camellia, who lived her life trying to find flaws within The Solution, still believed there had been a need for change; and whether or not this was the best answer, like everyone else she had come to accept it. I had never really thought about the head of The Solution, Dr Parisi, since grade school, where we studied his invention and learned about what had gone on to implement his practice. I didn't care one way or another about Dr Evil, but I do have some strong feelings about his grandson! Now that I know Milo had lied about his name, can I believe anything else he told me about his family? His mom was estranged from her dad, so does Milo know about his lineage? I guess that must be the cryptic message Miguel was trying to tell me: to find Milo, you have to first find his mom. His deceased mom. At least, I think she's dead.

***

After dinner, I'm surprised to find Mom lingering around the living room instead of rushing off to her bedroom, where she's been taking a heavy dose of sleeping pills and passing out. Tonight, as I clean up, I see her making goo-goo eyes at Violet in her baby chair and reaching out to squeeze her chubby thigh. While Dad jumped right into the grandparent role, Mom has been very stand-offish. Only holding or helping with Violet when I ask. She hasn't shown much affection or interest. I didn't want to push the issue, especially not so quickly after Dad's passing, but I tell Mom I need to make a phone call for a work project and ask if she could give Violet a bath for me. She seems hesitant at first, but after I fill up the kitchen sink and show her how I hold Violet in the water, Mom takes right over and is reminding me that she'd bathed me in this very same sink not too long ago. I leave the two of them in the kitchen and can hear my Mom humming the Rubber Ducky song as I shut my bedroom door.

My phone call isn't work-related; it is to Camellia. "Hey! How are you handling things? Is Mom driving you crazy yet?" she asks in one breath.

"No; she's been okay. Still sleeping a lot, but she went out and did some work in the greenhouse today, which I think is a good sign, right? And she has her game night with her friends tomorrow, so I'm hoping some social interaction will be good for her. She actually seems kind of interested in Violet for the first time tonight, believe it or not. I actually left her to give Vi a bath …"

"What? Do you think that's safe? Does she know how to bathe a baby? Has she taken medication tonight?"

"I don't think so. Jeez, you're freaking me out. Hang on, I'm going to go check on them." With no sounds coming from the kitchen, my pulse quickens as I walk through into the living room. There is no sign of Mom or Violet. I rush down the hall and push open Mom's bedroom door. The light is off and I bump my toe into the door frame as I scramble to turn the light on. Nothing. I hobble out into the hall and see the light on outside on the porch. I look out the window to see Mom sitting in the rocking chair, with Violet all bundled up in a towel. I can hear faintly through the glass as my Mom sings a lullaby.

"They're fine! I almost took off my big toe. Thanks for worrying me for nothing."

"Sorry. I'm glad Mom is doing okay, and that's great that she's spending time with Violet, finally."

"Yeah. It is. So, listen, I actually called you to ask you about something work-related. You know that database that The Solution uses to identify everyone and their vials? Do you guys have access to it with The Cause?"

"Why? Has someone said something about my behaviour after Dad died? Those assholes. We were perfectly within our rights to know…"

I cut Camellia off before she went too far into her rant. "No, no. No one has said a thing about you. I was just wondering more about the information they have on us and how up-to-date it is."

"Oh. Well, they have spent hundreds of millions of dollars on this database and as far as I know it's as current and reliable as you can get. But no, we've never seen it, I'm sure because they have information that is unethically sourced, so we've never been given access despite our best efforts."

"Oh, okay. Well, no worries, then," I say, trying not to hide my disappointment while keeping Camellia from prodding deeper into the real reason for my interest.

"But you know who *would* have access… Camden! Maybe you should give him a call." My sister says this in a teasing voice. "He seemed pretty happy to see you the other day. His aunt was asking me questions at Dad's celebration about your current situation. You have a few more weeks left at the farm, why not socialise a little to pass the time?"

I know exactly what Camellia is suggesting, and I'm not going to give her the satisfaction of agreeing with her. "Oh, wow, Camellia, I have a baby; the last thing Camden wants to do is spend time with his ex-girlfriend who shattered his heart and then became a pathetic single mother!"

After we talk for a few more minutes, I hang up the phone and once again peek out to see how Mom and Violet are doing. I'm surprised to see Mom has heated up a bottle from the fridge and has gotten Violet all dressed and ready for bed. When she looks over at me, I whisper that I'll just be one more minute. I quietly close my bedroom door and scroll through the numbers on my phone. Camden Conrad. I take a deep breath and press call. It rings three times and goes to voicemail. I quickly hang up, happy that Camden doesn't have my new number, so he wouldn't know who had called him, until suddenly my phone starts ringing and his name is on the display. Oh god, if I don't answer he'll hear my name in my voicemail message. What am I doing?! I decide to answer.

"Hi, Camden."

"Hi, I missed a call from this number; who is this?"

"Oh, sorry, yeah. It's Dahlia. How are you?"

"Oh, hey! Good. I'm good. How are you?"

"Really good. Well, you know, as good as can be expect... Umm, I just wanted to apologise for leaving so rudely the other day. I'm staying with Mom now for a few weeks and since I'm here I just thought maybe if you were free one night, we could grab something to eat and catch up. If you wanted. Totally fine if not."

"Wow. What's with the rambling?" Camden laughs. "I don't remember you being this awkward."

I finally exhale and laugh. "Yeah, I don't know what's gotten into me."

"Of course I'd love to catch up. How about Friday?"

"Yes, that sounds great. There's just one thing I should tell you. I have a baby. Her name is Violet. She's three months old. I don't know why you need to know that, it's just... well, I'll make sure my Mom can watch her, but Friday is good." Here I go, rambling again.

"See you then!" Camden says without skipping a beat.

Why was I so awkward? Maybe it's because I just called up my ex-boyfriend in the hopes of tricking him into getting me information about my missing boyfriend/baby daddy. Poor Camden. He's the last person in the world I want to use, but Camellia is right,

145

I might as well get back in touch with some old friends while I'm here. It will be nice to see Camden, and even if I'm not able to get anywhere with my search, I could use an adult night out.

Chapter Eighteen
Dahlia — 62 years, 3 months, 22 days

It was a Tuesday night; the one day I didn't work the evening shift serving at the pub in town. Camden was working as a landscaper that summer and since it had been raining for a week, he hadn't been working much. He was trying to save up enough money to rent his own place and move out of his parents' basement. We'd been dating all through high school and after graduation most of our friends had moved away; but neither Camden nor I had left, and that meant we'd only had each other for the past year. And while that seemed to suit him just fine, I was starting to feel restless. I had been taking online programming courses all summer long and had secretly applied to a college programme in the city and had been put on a wait-list. I hadn't told my parents or Camden, but every day I would rush to the mailbox before anyone else did to see if I'd received a response. On that rainy Tuesday, I had beat my Mom to the mailbox on my way home to change before going over to Camden's house to watch a movie, as we always did on Tuesdays. I couldn't believe it when I opened up the box and there was the letter I was waiting for, and in black and white was the word 'Accepted'. I barely processed the rest of the letter and just skipped right to the bottom where it said 'Classes start September 7th'. I had one month. I knew in that instant I couldn't wait one month. I had to leave now. This week. I had to start my life, and that meant leaving everyone behind.

When I got to Camden's house an hour later, I was surprised to see he'd ordered pizza for us and splurged on a bottle of wine. I was so used to his scrimping and saving every penny, this uncharacteristically extravagant meal was a huge surprise. When I asked him what the occasion was, he said he had some news. As I sheepishly swallowed down my wine, I thought of my own news and how I was going to broach it. Camden announced that he'd received his latest cheque for all his overtime last month and that he'd saved up enough to rent a place in the apartments off main street. He was rambling about how they weren't the nicest places in town, but it would be a start, and that if we fixed them up a little, we could...

"We?" I said. "You want me to help you decorate it?"

"No, I think you should move in with me. I know our parents won't be thrilled, but we're old enough to make that decision and we've been together for years. I'm sure they know it's only a matter of time before we're married, and so this is just the logical first step. Living together. It'll be so awesome."

Oh wow, I thought to myself. When did I fall out of love with this man? Was it ever love or just high school lust all along? Because sitting here in his parents' basement, picturing us bringing along this worn-out sofa and TV to our new (very old) apartment made me feel suddenly queasy. I had planned to come over tonight and explain to him all about my plans of moving to the city, and while I knew he would never come with me, I had planned on us staying together and figuring out a long-distance relationship; but all at once that window had suddenly closed. More like that door had slammed shut and was dead-bolted. I couldn't picture a life with him at all any more, no matter how wonderful a boyfriend he'd always been. He was too safe, too predictable and too boring. But how do you explain that to someone?

"Camden, I'm so sorry. I can't move in with you. I have some news of my own." I explained to him all about the programme I'd applied for and how prestigious it was. I'd been selected with just a handful of other people and would be training with the most elite coding experts in the country. I couldn't turn this down. I tried to explain how I'd needed to get out of this town. I'd stuck around after Camellia left years ago for my parents' sake, but it was my turn to live my life now.

"I can't move to the city, Dahlia, you know that. My parents only have a few years left. How could you even ask me to do that?" Camden looked over at me with hurt in his eyes.

"I didn't ask you. Actually, I'm not asking you. I'm sorry, but I think we want different things. You love this town and see a future here. I don't any more."

And that was it. That was the last time I saw Camden before he turned up on my parents' porch the day of Dad's death. I remember going home that night and having a huge fight with Mom when I told her I was leaving. The next day I hurt my Dad's feelings, too, when I screamed at him for just asking me where I was planning on living in the city. I boarded a bus on Saturday with just a suitcase and my computer and headed straight to campus and never looked back. I was quickly able to mend things with Dad, and I eventually gave my Mom a half-hearted apology; but I never did reach out to Camden again. I always figured he'd met some nice local girl and settled down. He deserved to be happy. I just knew I couldn't make him happy at the expense of my dreams.

Chapter Nineteen
Dahlia — DD in 54 years, 7 months, 13 days

"Thank you for meeting me here tonight," I say, as we sit at a small table for two in the dimly lit Italian restaurant that overlooks the lake on the north side of town.

"I'm glad you called. I felt so bad about showing up like I did the other day. I'm sure I was the last person you wanted to see that day."

"Well, I was surprised at first, but it was fine. You were just doing your job."

"How is your Mom doing?" Camden says, looking concerned.

"She's okay, I think. She's been preparing a lifetime for this, and now that it's done and he's gone, I don't think she thought as much about the after. She knew she'd keep up her plants as a hobby, but without the business she seems a little lost," I say, as I fiddle with the napkin on my lap. "She's bonding more with Violet than I expected. She was slow to warm up to the grandparent thing, but she's really come around now. It's been a really nice distraction, I think. She was thrilled when I asked her to babysit tonight. And she was so glad I was meeting you. She always liked you."

Everyone likes Camden. He is tall, polite and kind. He is exactly the kind of person parents hope their daughters would date. Date and hopefully marry.

"I must confess, I already knew about you having a daughter. My aunt was at your Dad's celebration of life and said she saw you carrying around a baby. So, I wasn't surprised when you told me over the phone the other day."

I'm not sure what I am going to say about Violet and my situation, but it doesn't seem like the time to launch into the whole missing Milo saga, and for some reason I don't want to. This is an evening out where I can just be the old Dahlia and not left-in-the-hospital-moments-after-giving-birth Dahlia. I decide to keep the conversation light and try to enjoy the evening.

"Tell me more about your job," I ask, as I rip apart a piece of focaccia bread.

"It's good. The Solution is a great employer and I like the responsibility of the Director role. I do get pretty bogged down with the paperwork and kind of miss the action of the enforcement side of things. But I still get called out to the odd unruly situation every now and then. 'Escalations' we call them."

"I'm sure you heard about my sister's escalation after Dad passed," I say, wondering what Camden might know about that incident.

"Yeah, that kind of thing happens more often than you'd think. People can be as prepared as possible for a death, but it still hits like a ton of bricks. Even someone like your sister who knows the ins and outs of our role in the matter, it's still an emotional time. I've seen it all. Just part of the job."

"Well, I hope they pay you well, because I couldn't imagine having to deal with that stuff."

"Nah, the pay is not great. Actually, I've gotten into real-estate in the last few years — that's where the real money is," Camden says with a smirk. "I've kind of turned this side of town into my own personal Monopoly board," he says earnestly, not meaning to sound like he's bragging. "First, I bought up the apartment building off main street. The one where I first rented after you left." Camden doesn't meet my eyes as he continues. "It was for sale for dirt cheap, so I bought it and turned it into a few condos and kept some as affordable rentals. It's been an amazing investment. I've done the same thing with a few other properties along this block. That duplex over there, and that strip mall," he says, as he points out of the window and down the road.

"Wow, that's really impressive, Camden. I've always been a renter. I've never had my name on a single mortgage. I can't imagine buying up a whole block!"

"It was all just good timing. But you know, I love this town, and it's been really rewarding. I can help keep rent low and provide quality places for people who really need it. Don't get me wrong, it's still a business," he says with a wink.

"So where are you living now, Uncle Pennybags?" I say.

"Excuse me?" Camden laughs.

"That's the Monopoly moustache guy's name!"

"No, it's not."

"It is. Seriously. I have no idea how I know that," I say, laughing.

"All right, I'll believe you. I moved into my parents' house after they died and have been slowly renovating it over the years. I thought I was going to flip it, but I don't think I can part with it now. It's always been home."

"So, no Mrs Conrad? I find that hard to believe," I say, trying not to seem as curious as I really am.

"Umm, no. Nope. Never made it that far. I was engaged a few years back, but it didn't work out. She didn't end up being who I thought she was."

"I can relate to that," I blurt out.

"So, Violet's Dad isn't around?" Camden asks quietly. That's an uncomfortable question to answer from your ex.

"He's around somewhere, but not exactly present with us at the moment." I gulp down the rest of my wine and change the topic again.

***

Going into dinner, I thought it would be a struggle to pretend that I was enjoying myself, but it's been so nice reminiscing I've surprised myself with what a good time I've been having. I don't know if it's butterflies or just old memories, but I'm feeling like a teenager again. I had felt suffocated in this town and needed a fresh start all those years ago, and I remember feeling suffocated by Camden's love, too, but I'm having a hard time believing that now. As I sit across from him, having finished half a bottle of wine by myself, more than I've drunk since Violet was born, I'm feeling warm and nostalgic and even flirty.

After we finish dinner, dessert and cappuccinos, Camden, always the gentleman, offers to drive me home. I look at my watch and see it's only 10pm. I'm not ready to let this evening end, and while I'm thinking it's because of how wonderful it feels to be around Camden again, I start to remember the reason I'm out with him in the first place. I need to get back to his place and try to get onto his computer and search The Solution's database. It is such a crazy plan and likely going to backfire, but it seems like the only option I've got.

"It's still early. I'm not ready to go home yet," I say, as I put my hand down on top of Camden's. He quickly moves it away and runs his fingers through his hair. "I'd love to see the renovations you've done to your parents' house. Could you show me?" I say in my most sultry voice. I can tell I have shocked Camden with my forward request, basically asking to go back to his place, but he is too sweet to turn me down.

"Uh, sure. Yeah, why not a quick tour, and then I'll take you home."

After half an hour of wandering around in a time warp of Camden's parents' home, we both sit down on the couch in the living room.

"The place looks so great, Camden. It still has all the charm it always did, but the renovations you've done are amazing. That extension out back really opened it up. The place feels so big now."

"Thanks. Yeah, I'm really happy with it, but it's a lot of space for just me," Camden says, as he unexpectedly slides over closer to me on the couch. "Dahl, I know you are going through a lot right now, but I just want you to know that I've loved spending time with you tonight. I had kind of blocked out all those feelings and memories when you left town, but seeing you again… I don't know. It just feels good. I haven't felt like this in a long time."

"I know what you mean. It's like those feelings never went away, they just kind of stayed buried deep down. It's hard to explain," I say, staring into Camden's familiar water-blue eyes. He's sitting really close to me on the couch now, and just when I'm sure he's going to lean in and kiss me, he jumps up. "I have something I want to show you. It's in a box upstairs in the attic. I'll be right back."

I rest my head back on the cushion and take a deep breath. I'm shocked at my feelings resurfacing for this man, but I suddenly realise I don't have time to analyse them now. This is my chance to see if I can get into Camden's computer. I get up from the couch and make my way over to his office. As I turn the door handle, I stop myself. I can hear Camden's footsteps up two flights of stairs and the sound of a creaky door opening. I lean my back against the office door and shake my head. I can't do this. I can't betray this man again. I'm going to have to find another way to track down Milo's mother. This is not right. I quietly close the door and sit back down on the couch.

After a few minutes, Camden comes back in the room carrying what looks like a piece of wood. "When I renovated and put the extension on the back of this house, I had to knock down some of the trees in the backyard. When this tree came down, I just couldn't part with this." Camden hands me the thick piece of bark. There, carved out in wood is C+D = heart. I can feel tears stinging my eyes. I'm a mess of emotions as I stare in the eyes of a man who saved a piece of wood for a decade as I come to the realisation that I've saved room in my heart for him all along. But in this moment, it's not only his face that I see, it's also the one that disappeared on me. As I try and pull myself together, I say, "I think it's time you took me home."

Chapter Twenty
Dahlia — DD in 54 years, 7 months, 10 days

It's been a few days since my evening with Camden, and I am still unsure about seeing him again. He's called several times and we've texted briefly back and forth. I just can't seem to sort out whether I am just reacting to the guilt I have about my intentions of meeting him in the first place or whether I truly still have real feelings for him. And if I do, what does it mean that I can so easily put aside my love for Milo like that. Am I just so hurt that he's left me and Violet that I am forcing myself to feel something other than pain and rage? Also, to top it off, I am living with my freshly-widowed mother, being reminded of my father's absence with every moment I spend at home. I guess it is no wonder I have no idea what my emotions are; I just have way too many to sort out. The easiest feeling to identify is the love I have for Violet. It is so overwhelming and complete. She is changing so much every day, from becoming more alert to starting to smile when she sees me. She is the only light in such a dark time. I am constantly reminded of what Dad said about moments: that you have to cherish the good ones, and move past the bad. There's nothing quite like spending your days with a beautiful, healthy baby to make you truly appreciate all the glorious moments, and I really am trying my best to let the sad and painful ones evaporate. Sometimes easier said than done. I think Mom is, too. She is spending more and more time with Violet and I notice a change in her, too. The three of us have found our own little rhythm and are taking things one day and one moment at a time.

It is the afternoon of the Lilac Festival, a big street festival that happens every May in town. Main street closes down to vehicles and local vendors set up booths. There is music, food and lots of flowers. It is the unofficial kick-off to the summer season. Violet and I have been making our way down the busy street as I struggle to navigate the stroller through the crowd. I notice the familiar names on the booths of shops and restaurants that have been here my whole life. It's amazing to me so much has changed, but this town has been frozen in time. I cross the street and come upon Mom's set-up for Dobbs's Greenhouse. I'm shocked to see she's sold out of almost everything.

"Wow, Mom. Business must have been booming. I guess people realised they'd better get it while they still can." I let this slip out before I realise the damage an innocent comment like this can have on my Mom. But she just turns and smiles, nodding her head while rearranging the few pots of geraniums still available. She seems to be handling her last Lilac Festival much better than I expected. Maybe the closing of her business is what she needs. Less pressure and more time to focus on what her life will be now. Life without Dad or her plants. Still seems unbelievable.

A couple of older women come in and start chatting with Mom about her flowers. That's when I notice Sara come in from the back. Sara was one of the young seasonal workers who had been working for my parents for years. She was back again this summer, but this time it was to help close out the business. I could see Sara sweeping out the spilled potting soil from under the tent.

"Hi, Sara. How are you? How is school going?" I say, as I push Violet's stroller back and forth, trying to encourage her to nap.

"Hi, Dahlia. School's great. Only one year left to go. I'm happy to be back home for the summer, though."

"I'm glad you were able to come back again. I appreciate you being able to help Mom out, especially this summer," I say quietly to Sara.

"Your parents have both always been so great to me. I've appreciated having a job to come home to every summer. I'll do whatever I can to help with closing out the Greenhouse."

As I'm chatting with Sara, Mom comes over and notices a sleepy-looking Violet in the stroller. She asks Sara to finish up things at the fair, and tells me she feels like a nice walk home. She'll take Violet, who will surely fall asleep on the walk, and wants me to enjoy the afternoon at the festival. I'm not going to argue, so I hand over the diaper bag and stroller and give Violet a kiss on the forehead.

"Be a good girl for Grandma, Vivi," I say, as I walk away along the sidewalk, feeling somehow lighter but also not myself with just my phone, wallet and a couple of hours alone. I try to embrace the freedom and turn the corner at the stop sign as I spot a real-estate booth set up across the street and unintentionally meet eyes with the man behind the bench. Camden! My gut reaction is to look away and pretend I hadn't seen him, but it is too late. He has seen me. I wave and make my way across the street over to him.

"Hi. How are you?" I say, trying to sound cool and calm.

"Aren't you missing someone? Shouldn't there be a tiny human near you at all times?" Camden says with a smile.

"She was here; Mom took her back home. She's giving me the afternoon off. I'm not even sure what to do with myself."

"How about you start with a coffee," Camden says.

Camden and I walk together down the street, coffee in hand. He's filling me in on all the gossipy details that come with small-town life. "Mrs Jefferson from Stan's Bakery is running the place alone now. Stan left with a much younger 'twinkie', to put it in Mrs Jefferson's terms. The place has never done better, though. Either she has a better knack for business than her husband ever did, or more likely, she was always running the show and now doesn't have him in the way."

I'm enjoying the simple chit-chat and the few encounters we've had with some old acquaintances.

"Camden and Dahlia! Well now, that's a throw-back!" We bump into an old friend from high school who gets a kick out of seeing us together. As we politely make small talk with him and his wife, Camden gets a phone call and excuses himself. "Officer Conrad," Camden says sternly into his phone. "I'm off today, but I can assist. What are the details?"

I can tell Camden's call sounds serious, so I also say a quick goodbye and follow Camden across the street a few paces behind to give him some privacy. I can hear him discussing some kind of disturbance that was called in and they are needing some guidance. I try not to be eavesdropping, but it's still hard for me to reconcile the passive, quiet guy I used to know with this serious official.

"No, Mackenzie doesn't have that kind of clearance. I'm a couple of minutes away from my place. I'll run home and pull up the file. I'll call you back."

Camden comes over to me and says that there is some kind of issue with work and he just needs to pull up a couple of things on his home computer. He tells me to come along, that it will only take a moment. We walk quickly back down the familiar tree-lined street towards his parents' house. Camden goes into his office and closes the door; he tells me to make myself at home, and as I sit down on the couch, those same feelings from the other night flood back over me. What am I doing here? Why am I so drawn back into him? My thoughts are interrupted by a loud siren followed by honking outside. I get up from the couch and look out of the window and see two police cars race by. I then hear Camden loudly on the phone yelling numbers and dates out to someone on the other end. "Code Delta Seven," he says.

Camden flings open the office door with one hand and is buckling on a belt with the other. The belt has several contraptions hanging off, including what looks like a gun.

"There's been an incident at the Festival. Stay here. I'll be back as soon as I can. Don't go outside."

Camden rushes out of the front door, slamming it behind him.

I sit back down on the couch and pull out my phone to call Mom. It rings and rings, as always with Mom, but she finally answers after what feels like an eternity. "Oh, thank goodness you answered. Where are you?" I yell. She says she arrived home half an hour ago and that she was able to transfer sleeping Violet from her stroller into her crib and she's been sleeping like an angel ever since. I tell her to stay where she is and that something is going on at the Festival and that I'll let her know when I hear more.

After I hang up with Mom, I start pacing the room. I'm feeling sick not being near Violet right now. I shouldn't have left her. She's just so little and I'm not sure I completely trust Mom in an emergency situation. I'm feeling sick with worry, trying to think of a way I could get a ride back to the farm, when I notice the blue light coming from Camden's office computer. I get up and walk over to the room and lean against the door frame. There, open on the screen, is a browser window titled 'Solution Database', with a blinking cursor next to a field that says NAME. Without even taking a second to think, I launch myself into the chair and type in MILO PARIS

NO RESULTS

Then I type: ISOBEL PARISI

Deceased.

Death Date Age: 41

ParColm Vial #7875 — Retrieved c/o AP<**>PM

Last known address: 653, 7th Avenue, The Core

I find a piece of paper and pen and frantically write down all the information on the screen. Then I type in MILO PARISI

MILO PARISI

Deceased.

Death Date Age: 7

ParColm Vial #16542 — Unretrieved

Last known address: 653, 7th Avenue, The Core

Deceased? At age seven? Am I wrong about Milo's identity? Maybe it's just a weird coincidence that he has Isobel Parisi's notebook in his loft. I fold up the piece of paper into my pocket and rush out of the office, glancing over my shoulder to make sure I haven't left any evidence I'd been in there at all. The adrenaline of what I'd just done finally hits me and my heart is pounding out of my chest as I sit back down on the sofa. I take deep breaths to calm myself down. After a couple of minutes, the front door opens and Camden walks in. He rushes over to me. "Are you okay? You're really pale," he says. My body feels numb now that I'm confronted face to face with Camden, and the shock of what I've just done and how terribly the timing could have been is now pulsing through my brain.

"Yes, uhh... I'm fine. I was just worried about Violet. It took me a little while to get hold of my Mom. They're safe at home," I say, trying to slow down my pounding heart. "I was just really worried about what was going on outside." It's terrible how easily I'm able to lie straight to Camden's face.

"Of course. Sorry, that took so long. I'm glad your Mom got home okay. A riot broke out at the festival. Some guy's vial is almost up and it looks like he wanted to go out with a bang. We were able to apprehend him before anything got too out of hand." Camden gets up from the couch as he's talking and walks towards the office. I watch him as he opens up the cabinet and hangs up his belt. He pulls a key out of his pocket and locks it up. I hold my breath as he looks down at the computer and I watch as he reaches down and switches it off and moves towards the door and turns off the light. I let out a deep exhale.

"Wow, that's crazy. I'm glad no one was hurt. I should probably get home now, though," I say.

"Okay. No problem. I'll give you a lift. I need to go into the office anyway," he says.

It's a quiet ten-minute drive back to the farm, with neither of us saying much. My mind is a thousand miles away and Camden seems distracted, too. As he pulls up the driveway, I can see Mom and Violet sitting out on the porch. I was hoping to avoid an awkward meeting between Mom and Camden, but before I even have a chance to ask if he wants to come and meet Violet, Camden is the one who cuts it short. I can tell he's thinking the same thing, although I'm not sure if it's Mom or the baby he's avoiding, but he says he'll give me a call soon, and before I've even let go of the door handle, he is in reverse, heading back down the driveway.

***

I'm sure Mom can sense my anxious energy all evening. Ever since I found the information on Camden's computer earlier, I just can't stop pacing. If Milo Parisi died at seven years old, then who is the Milo Paris that I supposedly know and love? I feel closer than ever to figuring this whole thing out; but, being stuck at the farm, I'm not getting anywhere. I head into the living room to give Mom a kiss before I turn in for the night and try to get some sleep. Mom closes the book she's reading, using her pointer finger to save the page, and I read upside down the words on the front cover: *On the Road: Surviving the Loss of a Spouse*. She catches my eye and looks down at the title.

"Joanie from the bank lent it to me. Her husband Martin died last year. She said this book really helped her grieve. Worth a shot, hey?"

"Good for you, Mom. I'm proud of you. But you know if you ever need to go back to Dr Melman's just for a tune-up, that will be okay."

"Thank you, dear. I hope it doesn't come to that kind of therapy again, but you never know with me." Mom gives my hand a squeeze and opens up her book again. Without looking up this time, she shouts after me just as I leave the room. "I forgot to tell you after all that commotion in town today. There was a voicemail left for you on our machine. I accidentally deleted it, but I did manage to write down the number. Guess it's pretty late now. You'll have to call them back in the morning," Mom says nonchalantly, and flips over the next page in her book as I come back into the room.

"What was the message?" I say, curious. Who would call this number to reach me? I haven't lived here for close to a decade?

"It said it was a message for Dahlia Dobbs and that this was listed as your primary contact number. Something about a reservation... no, that wasn't it. Resolut? No... Resolution! That was it. And they mentioned Milo's name, too. So strange!"

"WHAT? Mom! Why didn't you tell me this earlier? Where is the number?" I frantically start rummaging through papers on the island in the kitchen.

"I think I wrote it down on the grocery store flyer. I was cutting out a coupon when I listened to the message."

I toss aside piles of papers scattered all over the counter until, sure enough, I find the *Bill's Quality Market* flyer. In the left-hand corner at the top of the page, above this week's 'Produce Pickin's', is a ten-digit phone number written out in yellow highlighter. I bolt from the kitchen to my bedroom and come running back with the letter I swiped from Milo's loft. Sure enough, it's the same number from The Core for The Solution and its subsect 'The Resolution'. The same people who are trying to get a hold of Milo want to talk to me! My whole body feels sweaty, but I start to shake from the chills. Am I in danger now? Is Violet? What are we involved in? It suddenly becomes very clear to me that I need to go to The Core immediately, and maybe that will lead me to Milo somehow. The only clue I have is Milo's last known address from the database information I got earlier today. I'm supposed to be home with Mom for two more weeks, but I can't live in this limbo any more. I hope *On the Road: Surviving the Loss of a Spouse* is as good as Joanie says, because I need to hit the road myself, and figure out what the hell is going on in my life and what kind of shit Milo has dragged me into!

I start to pack my things to leave in the morning, and I am organising what I can, while Violet snores melodically from her bassinet. I start to group together all the files and loose papers of Milo's I'd been poring over for weeks that had been spread all over my room. I find the box in the corner that I'd grabbed from under his desk in his studio and am surprised to find it half full. I look inside and remember the pile of children's books still in there. I rummage through the box and count out seven books that seem to vary greatly in ages. The first book I notice is the same one that Milo had left in the hospital. It's a board-book for a small child, called *On the Night You Were Born*. I think it's funny that he'd have two copies of the same book. Maybe he'd forgotten he'd already bought that one. The next one I pick up is *Where the Wild Things Are*. I flip open the pages and see Max in the jungle with the creatures, and I remember reading this one so often as a kid. It had the best pictures. Next, I pick up a copy of *I'll Love You Forever*. I flip it open and see an inscription on the inside front cover:

Dearest Milo
Happy 4th Birthday my beautiful boy.
As long as I'm living my baby you'll be!
Mom

I start opening all the books' front pages, and sure enough there is a similar inscription on all of them: a birthday message, a poem or quote about reading, signed 'Mom'.

The last book I pick up is *Harry Potter and the Chamber of Secrets*. Inside the front cover it says:

Dearest Milo,
Happy 7th Birthday my handsome young man.
We are going to make this your best birthday ever.
Get your sleeping bag and hiking boots ready, *we're headed camping!*
Love you
Mom

Just as I'm about to close the book, thinking about Milo's mom and her sweet messages, out falls a very old, worn-looking business card. The card has scalloped edges and the front has an embossed logo. I turn over the card and it says 'Dr Paul Malcolm, The Solution, 100 1st Avenue, The Core'. I turn over the card and notice a small design on the back-left corner. I can barely make out the letters and symbols, but I recognise it from The Solution's database search I did at Camden's for the results on Isobel Parisi. An AP, two triangles, two stars and PM. These are all Milo's books given to him by his mom, and there are only seven of them. I think back to what I found on The Solution's database, where it said that Milo died at seven years old.

Is this a coincidence, or is it the biggest clue of all? Everything has been leading me to the city of The Core to solve this mystery of Milo's, and now I guess I have an actual target to track down. But am I really just going to waltz into the head office of The Solution and try to meet with the co-founder of the ParColm Vial?

Chapter Twenty-One
Milo — DD 0 years, 4 months, 13 days

I was supposed to die when I was seven years old. My mom and dead-beat-pompous-philandering father knew this. He only had to endure me for less than a decade and then I would be wiped clean like chalk off a blackboard. Of course, my mother was young and in love and was thrilled to have a newborn baby with the man she worshipped. I'm sure she thought it would strengthen their bond and solidify their relationship, and the fact that I would have such a short life just meant they would have to make the most of the time we all had together. I think it surprised my mother how much she fell in love with me, and that her need for my dad lessened. He would still come around from time to time and sweep her off her feet, and we would spend little chunks of time pretending to be a family; but then he would leave again and it would go back to just me and mom, just the way I liked it. My mom was a nurturing and loving mother, but if *he* was around, everything felt off. This cycle went on for seven years, until the day I didn't die.

The night of my death, my dad decided it was best for it to be just mom and me — no surprise there. Mom and I had spent the week before camping, and having never been told my Death Date, I just assumed we were having an awesome vacation. When we returned home, tired after a long drive, I couldn't believe it when mom said we could stay up and watch movies. We snuggled in close on the couch and I can remember my mom running her hands through the hair at the back of my neck for hours and not letting go of holding my hand. I asked her at one point why she was shaking and she said she was just cold. We cuddled up under a blanket and fell asleep that way. My mom was expecting to wake up the next morning to find her little boy cold and stiff beside her. First, she would call the authorities at The Solution and someone would come by to remove my ParColm Vial and a coroner would follow. Then she would call my dad, because she was sure he would want to say goodbye and she needed him there for support. That was as far as she could ever let her mind go. Even though she had seven years to prepare for this day, she was never able to process any thoughts past those two phone calls. How could she go on living after I was gone?

So, when she woke up the next morning in the blue light of the TV still on, she reached over to feel me lying beside her — but I wasn't there. She sat up, thinking I must have crawled into my bed during the night and died there all alone. As she got up from the sofa and started crying big, deep sobs, she rounded the corner of the living room to see me sitting at the kitchen table eating Cheerios and reading a Spider-Man comic book. She stumbled back into the wall and I asked her what was wrong. Was she feeling okay? Did she have another one of her migraines? She barely spoke a word and said she just had to check something. She bolted down to the basement and opened up the small fireproof box she kept down there and dug through piles of papers until she found what she was looking for. She had read this piece of paper a thousand times. It was worn down on the corners from being carried around in her bag for months after she got it. At my first post-natal check-up the nurse asked if she'd like to find out my Death Date and printed off the official copy for her records. There, in typed black and white:

Milo Parisi
Death Date Age: 7
ParColm Vial #16542

My mom calmly returned to the kitchen and with both eyes on me the entire time, she sat down across the table from me. I slid her over the box of Cheerios and asked what we were going to do that day. She had promised to take me back-to-school shopping and I wanted to get some new art supplies. We never made it to the store. By the end of the day Mom had packed up all our belongings and loaded up our SUV. We were moving. I had no idea what was going on, and when I asked if Dad was coming with us, she said no, we wouldn't be seeing him again. That was enough for me to accept this move without a fight. If this move meant I'd have my mom to myself finally, I wasn't going to object. Instead, I made it as easy for my mom as I possibly could. We settled into a new town a few hours away, changed our last name and after a couple of weeks at school, I made some good new friends and mom and I were happier than we'd ever been. At least, that's what I thought. I had no idea the inner turmoil my mom was dealing with each and every day. The emotional pain from her past, the physical pain from her 'migraines', the psychological torture of almost losing me and then the self-sabotage she hurled at herself in the form of alcohol and pills. I guess on some level I knew she wasn't well, but I was a self-absorbed kid and she kept so much of it from me, until the very end, when she couldn't cope with it all any more and I found her… dead. I also found her diary, and that explained everything!

**

The Diary of Isobel Parisi

Happy Sweet 16th Birthday to Me

Dad gave me this journal for my sixteenth birthday yesterday. He was probably hoping I'd use it for school work in the fall, but I've decided to make it my birthday diary. Since my Dad is in the business of stealing birthdays, I'm going to be the commemorator of them.

Besides, thanks to him, who knows how many I'll actually have! Better make the most of each one. I'll write in it every year around my birthday so I can look back and see what was going on that year in my life. Also, I feel like I need a place to get out all my feelings these days. Home life isn't exactly sunshine and rainbows. It's not like Dad has ever been super-involved, but he has crossed over into mad scientist territory. I hate this fucking custody agreement they came to. I wish I could just stay with Mom all the time instead of spending the summers with Dad. It's not like he even wants me around, or notices if I am. I can't even picture Mom and Dad together. I did the maths one day and they must have just been going through their divorce when Mom got pregnant! Gross. I don't want to picture that. Yuck! I have no idea how Mom can be so supportive of Dad. She's always coming to his defence, that he is a genius and that, sure, he lacks most basic social skills, she knows deep down he cares deeply for her and me. They met in their first-year college science class, and it was right around then when Dad started his passion project that has turned into his obsession, but it was Mom that helped him get it patented and make all the smart business connections. I think they probably just only ever spent time with each other so that's how they ended up together, but they must have realised they were better off as colleagues instead of as a couple. Mom is still running the business side of Dad's company and without her, he probably would have never succeeded.

I guess this journal is a good place for me to practice my writing, too. My English teacher, Mrs Simpson, thinks I have a knack for words and has been encouraging me to write down my thoughts, to see if it leads to any poetry or essays. I'm sure she's noticed how weird school has been for me lately. Being the daughter of Dr Evil hasn't exactly been easy on my social life. The closer Dad's damn invention gets to being a reality, the harder it is to make friends or keep the ones I've had. Everyone is so freaked out all the time about it all. Including me. I tried to have a normal conversation about it the other day with Dad and he just blew up at me. "This is my life's work, Isobel, and it's all about to be realised; your concerns are not quite my priority at this time."

So, I guess I will just wait out the summer holed up in my room with my books and then it's only two more years of high school until I can get the hell out of this city and go off to college somewhere where no one knows my family.

So… did I mention that when I said 'Dad gave me this journal for my birthday' what I really mean is that… he was at work — of course — and missed my whole birthday dinner. When he came home late with Dr Malcolm (so cute) to continue working in his study, I knocked on the door with a leftover piece of birthday cake. I wanted to make the old man feel bad and rub it in that he'd forgotten and see what he'd do about it. Of course, he wasn't fazed at all and clearly had no remorse. Classic. I was kind of hoping he'd whip out his wallet and give me cash to spend at the mall, but instead he just grabbed some leather notebook lying around on his desk and said this was my present and went right back to work. I hate him so much! It's a nice book, though, and it does have my initials inscribed on it (helps that Dad and I have the same ones!) And, I know Mom will feel bad and over-compensate for it at my party this weekend, so it's not all bad. Plus, I got to see Paul, aka Dr Malcolm, so I've had worse birthdays. And get this — Paul actually remembered! He came out of Dad's office while I was reading and said he was the one who suggested they leave their offices downtown and finish up work at our house. He said he never forgets my birthday because it's the day before his wife's (boo!), but then he gave me a 1920s edition of *Jane Eyre*. He remembered it used to my favourite! He said turning sixteen is a big deal and should be celebrated — that I'm turning into a young woman. I swear he said it in a hot way, not a creepy man way. I tried to act super-cool about it and just said thank you, but I was screaming on the inside. Maybe he really does like me?

17th Birthday
Another Birthday, another absentee father. This year, though, I'm glad he's not around. He's been doing so

much press lately about his damn ParColm Vial, that it's almost through beta testing blah, blah, blah, that it's going to save the world blah, blah, blah!!! Through all his noise, all everyone hears is that we're all going to start dying when he says so. Or when the Vial says so, I guess. It's the most depressing shit and it's gotten really scary. There have been all sorts of threats and violence. We had to move when some rioters figured out where we live and I had to start getting home-schooled after my principal was worried about my safety at school, as well as the other kids… (That part isn't actually so bad. I can learn all this stuff on my own anyways. I hated that damn school.)

With all the drama it seemed like even Mom was going to forget my birthday this year. She's been really stressed, too. I guess I would be if I were her. She's on the front line of all the press and appearances for The Solution. Dad and Dr Malcolm just hunker down in their lab at The Solution headquarters all day and only come out when there is some event they have to attend. I saw a video on the news the other day of people camped out in front of the building, harassing anyone coming or going.

Even though I've been staying with Dad (every damn summer!), Mom came and picked me up on my birthday and we went shopping, got our nails done, went to a super fancy restaurant and to a movie after. I was relieved when she didn't ask if I had any friends I wanted to invite along. I didn't have the heart to tell her all of the old girls I used to hang with have totally abandoned me. Not that I need them anyways. I have so much more time to read these days, and in a month, I'll be back at home living with Mom, I'll finish up my grade 12 course work early from home and DRUM ROLL… Mom said in the spring her and I can go on a month-long trip to Europe as a graduation present! I definitely want to visit Paris and London, of course, but maybe Prague and Rome, too! I can't wait!

The only bummer of my birthday celebration is that Mom dropped me back off at Dad's house at the end of the night. Boo. I told her to be careful going into work at The Solution. That it worries me. She said there is nothing to worry about. She's tough. A little peaceful protesting doesn't faze her. "I'm as strong as they come, Isobel. I was married to your father, after all. If I can put up with him, I can deal with anything!"

18th Birthday

We never did make it to Europe. Mom died before Christmas. Those peaceful protesters she said not to worry about got very out of hand. Mom got caught up in the crosshairs and a stray bullet.

"The bullet pierced straight through her brain; she was killed instantly. You should take comfort that she didn't feel any pain." Not exactly the words a teenager wants to hear from her Dad when she's found out her mother has been murdered. Murdered because of him. Everything that man touches is poison. And, of course, he just went right back to work. He said some bullshit about how she died for the greater good of humanity and she would have wanted to have his vision realised. "She was one of our soldiers, Isobel. We must keep up the fight."

I was going to defer my college entry for a semester after everything that happened, but I just need to leave this life behind and start somewhere new away from The Core. Everything here is ruined by Dad and anything good just reminds me of Mom, so I'm finally leaving it all behind for good.

19th Birthday

What a year! I feel like a totally new person now that I'm out of The Core and away at school. No one seems to care who I'm related to and I can finally just be myself. It's been the busiest year with school work and a social life. I could barely keep up.

I have made a big decision that after a year of general studies (Dad insisted I take it, hoping to steer me into sciences or maths — but at least he did pay!), I am switching over to Creative Writing. Dad, of course, is unsupportive and will probably cut me off at some point, but that is a chance I'm going to have to take. I think Mom would have been happy for me no matter what I decided to do with my life, so I'm going for it! Before Mom died, she took me to campus orientation. We sat in on a lecture from the Dean of the English Department, Dr Bernard, on "Rhetoric, Classical to

Enlightenment", and it was brilliant. I couldn't wait to take his "Intro to Poetry" in my first semester, and it did not disappoint. It completely inspired me to take my writing seriously and show that I could potentially even have a career from my words.

On my birthday I stopped by Dad's office to get a tuition cheque from him. I hate going into The Solution's building. It's so cold and uninviting and I just have horrible memories of what happened to Mom. Well, it turns out that Dad had left for some big conference, but I bumped into Paul Malcolm. He seemed really happy to see me and asked me a million questions about my college plans. He's always been way more into the arts than Dad, and actually appreciates the finer things in life. I have no idea how those two have anything in common. I guess just their Vial. The vile Vial! Anyways, Paul asked if I wanted to stay for lunch and his assistant put out a whole spread for us in his office. It almost felt like a date! He was telling me all about the different art he has collected over the years. He's so refined. Swoon. So, when lunch was over, he said he had to get going for an afternoon appointment, and as he walked me to the elevator, he was so sweet, telling me stories about Mom and saying how horrible he has felt for me. Such a compassionate guy. Anyways, he put his hand on the small of my back. I could feel tingles all up and down my legs. I never feel anything close to this when I'm with Jonathan in the back of his car. This was like real-deal electricity. So, I decided to just go for it and I leaned in and KISSED HIM! I can't even believe I'm writing this. I can't even believe it actually happened. And the craziest thing is, he didn't pull away. I mean, at least not at first. I could tell he wanted to keep going. I know he's married and everything, but it was just a kiss, right? He apologised after, like it was his fault. What a sweetheart. He's such a good guy.

Oh yah, and as far as birthdays go… Jonathan took me out on an actual date. It was nice, I guess. He's kind of boring and doesn't read, like at all, so we just don't have much to talk about. I don't think I'm going to see him any more.

20th Birthday

I definitely made the right decision in choosing my major. I have had the most incredible year and have never been happier. I'm doing pretty well in all my classes and maintaining a B+ average, but I did pull off an A+ in Dr Bernard's class. It could be because of my essay where I unpacked the nihilism in *A Clockwork Orange*, or it could be that he has fallen madly in love with me! Yes, you read that right! I'm some kind of young female college cliché, and I couldn't be more thrilled. I mean, aside from the sneaking in and out of his office at all hours of the day so we don't raise suspicion from his nosy secretary, who happens to be very good friends with his wife and also the godmother to his oldest son. Dr Bernard, or Bernie as I call him, is going to give me the job as his teacher's assistant next year, so we'll have more reasons to find ourselves behind closed doors and on top of his desk... on his chair... up against the bookshelf...

I mean, it's not like I didn't try and date guys my own age; it's just they all seemed so juvenile. I mean, none of them would ever even consider reading the classics, let alone reciting glorious passages from memory in bed! And oh god, the sex! It's like he's never satiated. He has opened me up to a whole new world of love-making. He's the most masterful teacher, and I am his obedient student. He's so tender and caring, it really is beautiful.

The only person in the world who knows about any of this is my dorm room-mate Samantha. She's in first year psychology; so, of course, she has diagnosed me with a Daddy complex. Well, that's just bullshit. Bernie is nothing like my father. He's open and communicative and available. Although he does also have a conscience (unfortunately), and, every once in a while, he'll want to cool things off for a bit. I know he goes back to his prude of a wife and tries to be happy with her, but he misses me and always comes crawling back. I've never asked him to leave her. What we have is so much bigger than marriage — we are soulmates, and nothing can, or will ever, change that!

21st Birthday

Dad insisted I come home for my birthday weekend this year. That he had some things he wanted to talk to me about. We've barely kept in touch at all since Mom died, and other than the cheques I get in the mail each month that remind me of him, he never crosses my mind. I've made a life away from all the labs and doom and gloom associated with that man. When I reluctantly went home and found him in his office, I was surprised to see him looking so happy and self-assured. I thought for the briefest second it was his reaction to seeing me, but no. He wanted to tell me in person that the ParColm Vial would be rolling out nationwide in a matter of months. That all HIS hard work and sacrifice was finally going to come to fruition. He said it was time for me to move home, as there will be even more media scrutiny than ever, and that the people at The Solution can keep a better handle on all things if I am here. When I told him NO, that I was happy at school and that I had a life there now, he completely dismissed me and said that I was wasting my time on "that useless literary shit" and that this wasn't up for discussion.

"You are one of us, Isobel, if you are not part of The Solution you are part of the problem, and I won't have one of my own blood jeopardising what I have built. Especially not now that we are so close."

I actually laughed out loud at his ridiculous comment, which enraged him even more. When I started to cry and told him I was in love and that I wouldn't be leaving, he asked with whom. I think I just wanted to make him mad, so I told him the truth. That I was in love with a married man twice my age and that I will never come back to The Core.

He sat down at his desk and drew in a long breath. He went very quiet and spoke just barely above a whisper. "Isobel, you have been nothing to me but a distraction and a disappointment in my life. It was your mother who wanted children, not me. I'm just glad she's not around to see your behaviour. To me you only ever got in the way. I never understood you, nor did I really care to. I am destined for greatness, Isobel, and what I am doing is going to change the world. All you'll ever be known as is the daughter of Dr Ignacio Parisi. You can stay in your pathetic life for all I care. I have brought two things into this world. One is a gift and the saviour of mankind — and the other is one that should have been aborted."

22nd Birthday

I haven't really felt up to celebrating my birthday this year. Bernie said he would take me away for a romantic weekend in the mountains, but I'm just not up for it. I'm trying not to care, but I guess I do. I learned about it on the news just like everyone else. "Dr Evil is Getting a Taste of His Own Medicine." Well, I'm not going home to see him. That's for sure. I have nothing to say to that man. He deserves to die. I hope he rots away into oblivion and is forgotten forever!

23rd Birthday

I had big plans for my birthday this year since the last couple of birthdays have been pretty awful; but ever since the car crash, I haven't been feeling well. I am so lucky none of us got more hurt, especially Stephanie, who was driving. I knew she'd had more to drink than she was letting on. We should have never gotten in that damn car with her in the first place. Somehow, me, with just a concussion, ended up in the hospital the longest, compared to Marissa and Melanie, who each had broken bones. Well, it turns out what they thought was a concussion was a brain bleed! I know, so scary! They caught it in time and rushed me into surgery. I was healing up okay at first, but now I just keep getting these insane migraines. I can't focus on anything. I barely graduated; if it weren't for Bernie helping me through those last couple of months, I don't think I could have made it. He was very sweet at first, helping me with my recovery, but he's been away with his family for most of the summer and I miss him. I just want to feel okay again. I have been taking so many medications for pain management and I just feel foggy all the time. There's been no way I could possibly write. It's like my creativity has been zapped. I'm so hopeful it will come back soon.

24th Birthday

Happy Birthday to me. This time next year I'm going to be a MOM! I can't believe it. I mean, at first, I was kind of freaked out. I took five pregnancy tests in a row. Bernie had a vasectomy years ago, so we never did use protection, but I guess we are just one of those one-in-a-million situations where a miracle gets through. Bernie wasn't exactly thrilled when he found out. In fact, it took him three days to call me back. Of course, I was heartbroken at first, but the more I thought about this little baby inside of me, the more excited I got. By the time he did call me back, there was no way I would even consider doing what he suggested, so I've made my peace with what will be our own little unconventional family and he will have to, too. I know he won't exactly be around as a traditional father, but mine wasn't either. For what it's worth, I don't think dads are all they're cracked up to be anyway. None of my friends ever had great dads. Even the ones who were around didn't seem to do anything. A good mom is what's most important, and I'll be a great one. I just know it. So here I am, on my twenty-fourth birthday, sipping ginger ale because little peanut disagrees with everything I try to eat or smell, and I couldn't be more blissfully happy if I tried. It's been hard for me to find a lot of joy in my life since Mom died. I don't admit it, but some days I feel like I just go through the motions. My old room-mate Sam (the Psychologist) used to call me a masochist. Like I welcome dysfunction. I thrive under strain. That's probably true. But not for long. This baby and are going to feel nothing but happiness and love!

25th Birthday

"On the night you were born, the moon smiled with such wonder that the stars peeked in to see you and the night wind whispered; life will never be the same."

Well, isn't that the truth? Life will never be the same. Ever since Milo was born at 2.31am on August 13th, my life finally has meaning and purpose and joy. He is the sweetest little baby. He is calm and curious and looks just like his dad. Speaking of Bernie, he's been around as much as he can, but he took a sabbatical and has been away for most of the year. He did help me get a part-time job as an editor, which has been really great. I'm still getting cheques from Dad's estate; I hate cashing them, but it was just as much Mom's money as it was his, and she would have wanted Milo and me to be comfortable. When Bernie does come back into town, we have the most wonderful time. I feel so happy with our beautiful little family of three, but when he leaves it's so hard.

26th Birthday

I spent my 26th birthday at the park with Milo. It was a beautiful sunny day and Milo was crawling around on a blanket I laid out for us. We were having a lovely time until I saw Bernie's secretary Rita walk by. I tried to avoid eye contact, but she spotted us and came over.

"This must be Milo," she said, with a menacing look on her face.

"Excuse me? How did you know that?" I said. I was completely flabbergasted! I thought Bernie and I had been discreet, at least for the last few years. We'd moved our rendezvous off campus after I graduated and Bernie would just come over to my apartment.

"Oh, dear Isobel. I've always known. That's part of my job, you see; it's not just Dr Bernard's professional affairs I tend to — I also had his personal indiscretions to handle. Those usually take up most of my time." The coldness and smugness coming off this woman was pungent. I couldn't even form a sentence. She had shocked me to my soul. What did she mean, indiscretions? Are there others?

"I'm sure you think you're special, don't you, dear?" I swear, if she called me dear one more time, I might have slapped her! "Dr Bernard has always enjoyed the perks he felt came with the job. I must say you have hung around the longest and have made your presence more permanent than the others." She looked directly at Milo as she said this, and that's when I stood up and lunged myself at the garbage can beside us, and I threw up all of my lunch.

"Oh my! Don't tell me you have morning sickness! One accident was enough of a mess to clean up. Dr Bernard can't afford to keep increasing my salary every time he makes these kinds of mistakes."

As I wiped off my mouth with the back of my shirt, the only thing I could think to say was, "Does his wife know?"

"Know about you or the baby? Definitely not the baby, I've made sure of that. And I intend to keep it that way." I'm sure she meant that as a direct threat. "And about you? Oh, probably. Or at least some version of you. There have always been floozies hanging around that pathetic man, but she knows they all have their seasons until he tires of them and comes back to her. I expect a change in season will be coming sooner than later." And then she walked away.

Needless to say, I was absolutely stunned and heartbroken. I feel like such a fool. All those years spent with this man. I really thought what we had was special. I know I'm a hypocrite, because I knew he was married, but we had a bond even stronger. At least I thought we did. Now I don't know what to think. To find out there have been other women… other students!!! It's so hard to process. I feel lost and alone. Although, I'm not alone. I have my beautiful baby boy.

27th Birthday

I wasn't going to find out Milo's Death Date. I have never wanted to have anything to do with the Vials or The Solution. I have always thought I would just live my life to the fullest and when I die, I die. No regrets. That's what I wanted for Milo, too. Bernie had a different idea. Things haven't been great between us all year. Ever since I confronted him about my encounter with his secretary last year, he has admitted to several affairs with his students. He assures me he was never in love with any of them and that what he has with me is totally different. He's even promised to leave his wife as soon as his sons are out of the house. (I feel dumb even writing that; it makes me seem so gullible, but part of me believes he will!) Or at least I did believe him, and I really did trust him… until my birthday. He surprised me by wanting to spend the day with Milo and sending me off to the spa for some much-deserved RnR. Having a two-year-old basically on my own has been exhausting and I couldn't believe how thoughtful it was of Bernie. I also loved that he wanted some quality time with Milo, who he hasn't really bonded with as much as I had hoped. Well, it turns out it was all a giant sham to get Milo's ParColm Vial scanned. Bernie couldn't handle not knowing, and he knew I would never agree to have him tested, so behind my back he had a doctor friend of his scan my boy without my consent! I was livid when I found out and haven't spoken to Bernie for two weeks. I can't bring myself to open the envelope he left behind and find out when my boy is going to die. The whole situation is wrapped up with the issues I had with my Dad, how my Mom died and now my son. It's just all too much for me to handle, but it has me very concerned, because Bernie won't stop calling me to talk about it. His behaviour is extremely unusual. He usually avoids confrontation at all costs and would typically just disappear for a while and let me calm down, only to re-emerge and sweep me back off my feet. He's really perfected the 'absence makes the heart grow fonder' routine; but not this time, so I'm terrified what is written on that paper must be really bad. Ignorance has always been my bliss, but now I'm just really scared.

28th Birthday

I have three more birthdays with my son. He is a Vitam Non-Vixit, 'a life not lived', and he will die when he is seven.

31st Birthday

Somehow, Milo is still alive and I have no idea how to keep him that way. Except to run far away and start over somewhere new. I am so terrified that someone will find out and kill Milo. This has to be tied to The Solution somehow. If it's a mistake, we can never let anyone find out; and if it's intentional and that someone is trying to hurt me and Milo because of who my dad was, then all the more reason why we need to disappear. Luckily, the only person who knew Milo's DD, other than me, was Bernie, and he assumed Milo died when he was supposed to. I sent him a letter saying that I couldn't see him any more, that he reminded me too much of Milo. He must have bought it, because I haven't heard back. To be honest, he was probably relieved that whole chapter of his life is over. I can't even think about that any more. It all seems so frivolous. Now all that matters is that I still have Milo and I am going to do everything in my power to keep it that way.

35th Birthday

I forgot all about this book when we moved, until I unpacked an old box and found it lying in the bottom. I'm sure it's cringe-worthy for anyone to read their teenage diary, but mine seems especially sad and disconcerting — all the pain with my dad, the loss of my Mom, my weird crush on Paul Malcolm, and, of course, my unhealthy relationship with Bernie! It's a lot to revisit and remember. I wish I could say I was doing really well, but that's not entirely true. I'm still in a lot of physical pain with my migraines after that car crash years ago in college, but I'm taking it day by day. I'm still so paranoid we are going to be found out. It causes me so much stress. I know I drink more than I should these days, but only after Milo goes to bed, so I don't think it's affecting him at all. He seems to be thriving! He's growing up so much and is doing great in school. He's got a great group of friends, including Oscar Lopez, whose family has really welcomed us into their own. I'm so grateful for the support from Maria and Miguel, but I can't help feeling guilty around them: Oscar's older sister Carmen died last year at thirteen years old. Their family is religious, so they don't know anyone's Death Dates, so it was a complete shock to wake up one morning and find her lifeless in her bed. My worst nightmare, the one I dreaded that was supposed to be my reality three years ago, actually happened to them. I have no idea how they cope with life. I guess they have to for the sake of their three other beautiful children.

We really have created a community for ourselves here and I'm so grateful for it. I've been working at the local library, which I love, and I also started really getting into cooking, which is great since Milo eats everything in sight. We cook together most evenings and it's such a special time for me.

I still have never gotten back to writing. I lost it around the same time as the car crash. It was like I woke up in the hospital and was missing that part of me. I don't even read like I used to. It makes me sad when I think of it too long, but I try and not dwell too much on the loss in my life; instead, I focus on the gratitude. I'm grateful I have Milo when I wasn't supposed to.

36th Birthday

I'm full of shit. Reading what I wrote last year, it's BS. I'm not okay. I'm sad and lonely and I drink myself to sleep every night. When I ran out of the pills my doctor prescribed me for my migraines, I started buying them off some creepy guy who comes into the library just to stay warm. How did I become this person? I mean, I can trace most of it all back to my childhood traumas, but I feel like it's gotten worse ever since Milo didn't die. I should be so happy all the time, and I say it out loud to myself almost daily: "YOU SHOULD BE HAPPY!!!" — but I'm just numb. I think of poor Miguel and Maria and their daughter Carmen who did die. That should be enough to shock me back to my senses, but it isn't. I know I should talk to someone. A therapist or something; but I can't tell anyone what my real problem is — that my son was supposed to die and he didn't, and I've been trapped in some horrible limbo since that day and don't know how to crawl my way out. I also have migraines that burst through my brain like a sledgehammer and so I drink or get high until I pass out, and then another day starts again and it's all the same. Fear, pain, sleep. Repeat.

37th Birthday

Maria threw me a birthday party. It was very sweet of her. It was just her family and Milo and me, but it was so kind and thoughtful. She made the most delicious three-layered chocolate cake. I wish I could remember more from that night, but I blacked out. Milo hasn't talked to me for a couple of days. I think he must have had to get me home. Maria assures me it was fine, that we all over-indulge on our birthdays, but I can tell she's not telling me the whole story. My poor boy. I must have embarrassed him so much. He doesn't deserve this. No one does.

40!!!! Fuck 40

I don't even recognise myself any more. I had so many dreams. So many plans. I need to be better for Milo. He deserves better. But how? The pain is too strong. So much stronger than I am. I'm so tired.

41st Birthday

This is the year I'm going to get it together. I'm on the back nine, as they say. Best-case scenario: if I got one of the good Vials from my Dad's damn invention, I could have another forty left in me. I want to see Milo grow old. I want to watch him find his own path to happiness. I want to see him fall in love and find a partner, even maybe have his own kids. I want to get better and be there for all of that. Who knows, maybe there is still a chance for me to find love and happiness, too? I know I can't do this alone and I need help. This is the year I'm going to do it.

Chapter Twenty-Two
Dahlia — DD in 54 years, 7 months, 8 days

I woke up this morning feeling confident about my decision to leave today. I broke the news to Mom over breakfast. She cuddled Violet in her arms and was understandably emotional. We'd talked a lot about her coming to visit in the city, that I have a spare bedroom and she could see Violet whenever she wants. That seemed to help. I know she has a lot of grieving still to do, but I have a good feeling she's going to be okay. She didn't ask many questions about where I am headed, but I'm sure she has her assumptions. Maybe Dad did tell her more than he let on.

As I pack up Dad's truck, I text someone else I have to say goodbye to. "Can you meet me at the diner for lunch?" I send the message and feel a lump in my throat. Mom offers to watch Violet while I go into town, but this time I want her with me.

**

"Hey! So, this is Miss Violet. She's beautiful, Dahl," Camden says, as I slide into the booth across from him.

Violet is asleep in her car seat and I put her down on the bench beside me.

"Thank you. I thought it was time you guys should meet. I know it's kind of awkward."

"It's not. I know I acted weird dropping you off the other day, but just seeing your Mom holding your baby. I don't know. A lot of stuff has been brought up this last month. I'm just trying to process it all, I guess."

"For me, too. That's why I called you today..." Just as I get up the nerve to explain my plans, Camden interrupts me.

"Hey, I see you're driving your Dad's truck. It kind of suits you."

"Really? I feel like a little kid driving it, but he wanted me to have it, and it's like he's with me somehow when I'm in it, so I kind of love it."

The waitress comes over and takes our order: we both just order coffee. I guess neither of us have much of an appetite with what's on our minds.

"Listen, Dahlia, I want you to know that it's been so great seeing you again. And I feel like maybe the time we were apart was meant to be, or something. As hard as it was when you left, maybe it was what you needed to do so you could appreciate being back. Realise maybe you left some things behind."

I can see in Camden's eyes what he's trying to say, and I know where this conversation is going, but I don't know how to tell him — again — that I have to leave. I can't seem to get up the nerve to cut him off, and so I just let him continue, astounded by what he's saying.

"I know you have a lot on your mind, with everything, but I just want you to know that we could figure this out; us, I mean… well, us and Violet. I would want that." Camden looks down at the table as the waitress drops off our drinks. I'm so grateful for the break in intensity while she puts down milk and sugar and asks if we want anything else.

"No, thank you," I say quietly. "Camden, I know how you feel because I feel it, too; it's just…" I am cut off by the sound of the diner door opening with a chime and the feeling of heavy footsteps behind me.

"Dahlia!"

I whip my head around at the sound of my name and the voice saying it. Low, gravelly and intense. I am stunned by the sight of the face that haunts me. The face I see every time I close my eyes, and the same face I see when I open them and look at my baby girl.

"MILO!" I jump up immediately and run into his arms. I fold into him, so grateful he is okay, completely forgetting about the hell he has put me through for the past month. Before I have a second to ask him what he's doing here, Camden gets to his feet.

"So, you're Milo. What the fuck are you doing here?" I am shocked at Camden's tone and choice of words.

"Excuse me? And who are you?" Milo releases me from his arms and moves towards Camden. Just as they get within an inch of each other's faces, Milo catches a glance down towards the booth bench and sees Violet. His face completely crumples and he backs away from Camden.

"Oh my god. Look at her. Dahlia, she's changed so much." I can see tears filling Milo's eyes, but I am totally frozen in one spot. I can't move, I can't speak, I am just a witness to this scene, as it plays out between my ex-boyfriend and my daughter's father.

"Don't you dare touch her." Camden breaks Milo's gaze on Violet with his threat.

The building tension eventually releases me from my frozen state. I tell Camden that it's okay. Could he please just stay with Violet for a minute while I talk to Milo outside.

As we get out to the parking lot, I start shrieking at Milo. "I can't believe you're here. How did you find me?"

"I went to the house. I saw your Mom. She told me. Who's the guy, Dahlia?"

"Camden? He's just an old friend. I don't think you have any right to be asking me questions right now," I yell, as my heart begins racing and pent-up frustration starts boiling over.

"I know you're mad. I'm so sorry. But I'm in trouble. I'll explain everything. I think I know who can help me. I was going to go alone, but I couldn't be apart from you or Violet another day. I might put us all in danger, but I had to risk it."

"What kind of danger? Who can help you? Dr Malcolm?" I say with a guess, remembering the name on the card that fell out of one of Milo's childhood books.

"YES! How did you know that? Has someone contacted you?" Milo pulls my arm forcefully, pushing me back beside the building, as he looks around suspiciously at the parking lot. Milo's eyes are darting from side to side. He looks so gaunt, he's lost a lot of weight and he hasn't shaved in months.

"When I didn't hear from you, I went poking around your place. I found that name tucked inside an old book."

Milo seems relieved by my answer.

"Where have you been? You look terrible. Are you feeling okay? You only have about three months left, is that right?" I seem to have caught Milo off-guard, mentioning his Death Date.

"Umm, yes, three months. That's right. Dahlia, how many people have you told about my Death Date?" Milo looks me straight in the eye as he asks me.

"No one, actually. I didn't really think it was anyone's business. It was sad enough that you left me and your newborn baby; people felt sorry for me as it is, so I didn't need to add to it the fact that you'll be dead soon, too!" I said, meaning every single sting of the words as they came out.

"Dahlia, I'm sorry. I will explain it all. We just have to go. Now!" Milo says, as he starts to make his way back towards the restaurant door.

"Why would I go anywhere with you after what you've done? I don't even know you. Everything you ever told me is a lie, Milo!" I say, as I start to cry. "I know about Isobel Parisi. Miguel helped me figure that one out. Was that part of your plan? Once you were dead, I'd figure out the truth behind my daughter's family, who her great grandfather was. Why would you keep that from me?"

"It was all to protect you. Everything I ever did was to protect you, but it didn't seem to matter. I ended up hurting you anyway." Milo tries to grab my hand as I back away from him. "I think I've figured out how to fix everything, but I need you and Violet with me. I don't want to do this alone."

I can see the pain in his eyes and something in me finally breaks. I have wanted to be back in this man's arms for months. I've dreamt about it every single night. I was on my way to find him, after all, so why am I making this so difficult?

"Dahlia. Please, you have to trust me. Go get Violet and get in my car. I'll tell you everything!"

"NO!"

Milo just stands defeated with his head down, like he has no fight left.

"We'll take my truck. I've already packed. I was leaving today. I was coming to find you. Just give me a minute to say goodbye to Camden."

***

"Hey," Camden says reluctantly. "Things looked pretty intense out there. Everything okay?"

"Yeah, it's all right. Just lots of questions, I guess. Listen, Camden…"

"You're leaving. I know. I knew it when I got here and saw your truck all packed up."

"But why would you say all those things before if you knew I was leaving?"

"I didn't put up a fight the last time you left. I've regretted it every day since. And then you showed up again and I wasn't going to let history repeat itself; but then *he* showed up." Camden takes a deep breath and gets up out of the booth. "It's okay, I understand. Just take care of yourself, Dahlia, and Violet, too."

I get up to give Camden a hug that he only partially returns. "I'm so sorry, Camden. I care about you so much and my feelings were real; it's just…"

"I know. We've been down this road before. No need to rehash that again. It's all good." Camden walks out of the restaurant and I see him give a sideways glance to Milo as he starts down the street, with his hands in his pockets and his head hung low. Somehow, I've managed to break the same sweet heart twice. I feel my own chest tighten as I watch him walk away. What I have done to him isn't fair and he doesn't deserve this, but sticking around town and pretending to play house with him would never have worked. I knew that a decade ago and I know it now. I should have left the past in the past.

I come out of the restaurant with Violet still peacefully asleep. I put her in the back seat of Dad's truck and Milo heads for the driver's side. "No, I'm driving. I've been a passenger to this saga for too long. I'm calling the shots now."

Chapter Twenty-Three
Dahlia — DD in 54 years, 7 months, 8 days

Milo and I drive for an hour, talking about my Dad's death and how my Mom is doing, but mostly all about Violet. I tell him about how much she weighs and how she's been sleeping. He has millions of questions as he flips thorough the photos on my phone, taking in all the moments I've captured of Violet that he has missed.

"Believe me, I'd love to talk about nothing but Violet, but I need to understand what is going on with you, and why you left."

Milo fills me in on all the details of his seventh birthday and the weeks that followed when he didn't die. I am completely shocked and have a hard time focusing on driving.

"This is unbelievable. I've never heard of someone not dying on their Death Date! Have you ever had your ParColm Vial scanned?"

"Just that day in the hospital when Violet was born," he says, looking out the window. "Well, and almost at your sister's house that one night, remember?"

"Oh, yeah. You got food poisoning? Or wait, you said you thought it was an allergic reaction to avocados."

"Yes. That's what I said."

"Not allergic?"

"Not at all. I've really missed eating them this year, trying to keep up that charade," Milo says with a chuckle.

"I'm glad this is all so amusing to you," I say angrily.

"I'm sorry. It's just such a relief to be able to talk to you about this now. I've kept this secret my whole life. And other than the bits and pieces I told Miguel and your Dad to get messages to you, this is the first time I've ever even talked out loud about it!"

"I understand. So, you didn't die when you were seven like your Death Date certificate said; but based on the vial scan at the hospital, you have, what, three months left?"

"Four months and eleven days. But that's the thing: I don't think I'm going to die then, either."

I take my eyes off the road and stare at Milo in disbelief.

"Dahlia, watch out!" Milo screams, as I look back at the road and realise, I've swerved into the other lane.

"You know what, let's pull over for a bit. There is a rest stop coming up. I need to feed Violet anyway."

***

We set ourselves up a picnic table as the afternoon light is just cutting through the tree's canopy. I am holding Violet up to my chest, feeding her like I have for the past three months; but I feel oddly uncomfortable with Milo watching me. He was the person I was most at ease with in the entire world just a few short months ago, but now I feel like we're strangers as he doesn't take his gaze off me.

"You are such a natural with her. I knew you would be," he says.

"It wasn't always like this. We took a while to get to know each other," I say, looking down at my sweet girl. It's already hard to remember those first few days, how we managed on our own. And then I think about Maria, how she was my anchor then.

"Miguel and Maria should be getting home from their trip soon," I say. "I've missed them so much. I couldn't have made it through those first couple of months without them."

"That's not what Miguel told me," Milo says. "He told me he was amazed at how strong you were for everyone."

"When did you see him, exactly? That book that you had him give me, when did all of that happen?"

"A few weeks after I left. I'd been staying a few towns away, trying to figure out what I was going to do, and I remembered some old boxes of my Mom's stuff that I had at my studio. I went back one night to get it, but it was all gone. I knew it must have been you trying to make sense of everything, and I just felt so guilty and I missed you so much. I couldn't handle the pain I was putting you through. So I went by Miguel's work shed late one night. His light was on and I knew Maria wouldn't be out there at that hour. If she saw me, I knew she'd kill me before my Vial ever had a chance!" Milo and I both laugh.

"I didn't want to burden Miguel with much of my situation, in case anyone ever did come asking; so I just told him to give you the book. He told me you and Violet were doing okay and that they were helping, but I knew that could only last so long too…" Milo trails off as we both think about the upcoming deaths of our sweet friends.

I'm lost in my thoughts when Milo asks, "Can I hold her, Dahl?" He looks so sheepish as he asks and I realise I've been holding Violet tight against my body this entire time, like I'm protecting her from him. Like the pain he's caused me will infect her. I think about how, regardless of what happens with us, she may only have a couple of months left with him, and I need to put my own feelings aside for my daughter.

"Oh, yes. I'm sorry!" I pass Violet gently over to Milo and immediately a big smile spreads across her tiny face.

"Hi, sweetheart. Hi," Milo says, as he nuzzles his head into her neck. I look away as the tears sting my eyes. The instant connection, these two share, is palpable. It's a connection I had expected the second she was born and one that I presumed would last an entire lifetime. Instead, it was stolen away before it ever had a chance, and now could only last a matter of weeks. I take a deep breath and try to steady my emotions. I have spent enough time these past months dwelling on what we've missed; my little family is together now and we have to figure out what to do to keep it that way. As Milo bounces Violet on his lap, I try to focus back on our task at hand.

"Has anyone from The Resolve tried to contact you?" I say, remembering the letter I found at Milo's loft and the phone call I received on my parents' answering machine.

"Resolve? No, I don't think so. I haven't exactly been reachable. Why, what's The Resolve?"

"I don't really know, but they left you a letter at your studio right after you left. I kind of stole it and opened it." I look over at Milo remorsefully, but he doesn't seem fazed. "And then the same people left me a voicemail message to call them back. It seemed really important. It's some sub-sect of The Solution; it seemed kind of threatening. Maybe I'm being paranoid."

"No, you're not. Actually, for the first few weeks I was in hiding, I was convinced I was being followed. I kept seeing the same car with the same guys in it. I swear they were on my trail everywhere I went."

"Shit, Milo. What the hell do they want with you? Do you think somehow at the hospital when Violet was born, your Vial scan alerted someone?" I say frantically.

"I don't know. I have no idea what to think any more," Milo says with a sigh.

"Okay. We'll figure this out," I say, trying to channel the calm I had in a crisis the other day with Camellia. "It's okay. So, tell me, why is it you don't think you're going to die in a few months like your scan said?" I say directly.

"I think my Mom knew something she didn't tell me. The night before she died, she was very messed up on pills and alcohol; she was rambling on and on about how all her problems started after my grandfather died. She was in some kind of car accident in college and when she left the hospital her headaches started and just got worse and worse over the years. She thought it was some kind of conspiracy, that someone was trying to hurt her because of who her dad was, and then she was sure when I didn't die when I was supposed to that they were going to hurt me, too. She was always so insistent I never have my ParColm Vial checked, and I avoided it until Violet needed blood. I know she never understood why I didn't die that night when I was supposed to, but she knew enough about The Solution, having been the daughter of the inventor, that she couldn't tell anyone about it. That's why we moved so quickly. My Dad also knew my Death Date, and if he knew I hadn't died he would have turned us in and they would have killed me on the spot. She figured our best chance was starting new somewhere, changing our last name and avoiding doctors and the authorities forever."

"Did you know what was going on then when you were a kid, that you didn't have a Death Date?"

"No, she didn't tell me right away; but I eventually figured it out. She had started drinking pretty heavily after the move. I think she missed my Dad a lot and the whole weight of the situation must have just hit her hard. She probably felt guilty, like she should be thrilled that she had me alive when I shouldn't be; but maybe the hiding and the risk of being discovered was too much for her." Milo stares off into the distance as he talks. He isn't looking at me or Violet, just saying out loud a story I'm sure he's played over in his head a thousand times.

"It wasn't long before the drinking led to pills, and those made her paranoid. She thought everyone was after us. That's when the whole story finally came out — in one of her messed-up states, I pieced everything together. I found my Death Certificate and realised why we had run. When she was drunk or high, she'd talk a lot about my grandpa and her issues with him. He was a brilliant scientist, but he didn't have any time for his family. The night before she overdosed, she was crying about some memory of her Dad and how he'd forgotten her sixteenth birthday, but his partner, Dr Malcolm, had remembered and brought her a present. I was half-listening at this point, but I remember her saying that if I was ever in any real trouble, that's who I needed to find, that Dr Malcolm would help me. After that, she passed out on the couch and I went up to bed. I had basketball practice before school the next morning, so I was up early, and when I came downstairs, Mom was still asleep on the couch. I tucked the blanket around her and kissed her on the forehead. When I came home from school that afternoon, she was lying on the kitchen floor with a pill jar in one hand, surrounded by all the books she'd given me as birthday presents as a kid. One for every year I was supposed to be alive. I remember so clearly, my first thought was that I knew she was dead before I even touched her, and strangely my second thought was wondering why she stopped at seven books. Why didn't she keep going? I kept having birthdays. It occurred to me then that I had kept living, but that same year she had started dying."

"That's so sad. She must have been in a lot of pain to be so self-destructive. You must have always wondered what she was thinking."

"I did at first. I would replay everything in my mind. Every conversation, every time she was drunk or high, I'd try and remember what she was upset about; but I never had any real insights... until I found her diary."

"Her diary?"

"When I was moving away to college a year after she died, I was cleaning up the house to get it ready to be sold. I found her diary beneath some books in her nightstand. It took me several days before I got up the courage to read it. It was extremely painful to read all her inner thoughts," Milo says.

"I can't even imagine. What did it say?"

"Well, it started when she was just a teenager. She hated her Dad, and then her Mom died. She had to deal with a lot even from a young age. There's a lot about my asshole Dad, and then she had me." Milo's voice starts to crack and I can tell he's about to cry. "Then she seemed really happy for a while. I think I made her really happy. But then when I didn't die, it just messed her up. She should have got help. I wish I could have known. If she'd only talked to someone." Milo trails off.

"Well, she probably knew she couldn't talk to anyone. It's not like she could go see a shrink and say 'my kid's ParColm Vial didn't go off when it was supposed to and now, I'm living every day worried someone is going to find out and kill him anyway'." I look at Milo, worried I've crossed a line with my bluntness, but he nods with me in agreement.

"After I finished reading her diary, I got really upset and tore all the pages out of it and burned them! I regret that now. I mean, the pages about my DD were a liability, but the ones where she was really happy… I wish I could re-read them."

"Was it a leather book? Did it have the initials I.P. on the cover?" I say, curiosity in my voice.

"Yes, why?"

"I found it in your loft. A leather notebook with all the pages missing. The initials on the front cover was the clue that finally made sense to me about this whole situation. Thanks to Miguel's tip off and that notebook,

I understood who your Mom was and who your grandpa was. It led me on the path to start finding you. In some weird way, that old diary brought us back together. It brought you back to Violet!"

Milo looks down at Violet in his arms and kisses the top of her head. We sit in silence for a while and just quietly enjoy the little smirks and movements Violet makes as she cuddles on Milo's chest.

My unsated curiosity about Milo's life and his Mom breaks our quiet moment. "Did you ever find out what your Mom's Death Date was?"

"No. At least, she never told me. As I got older, I kind of wondered if she had been grouped in with the nepotism scandals that happened in the early days of The Solution. Being the daughter of the inventor probably had some perks. I was never around if she ever did have a scan, so I don't know for sure, but I doubt she was supposed to die at forty-one."

"So, what did you do once you found her on the floor like that?" I ask cautiously, unsure of how he will react to such a delicate subject.

"I sat with her on the floor in the kitchen for a long time before I finally got up the nerve to call the authorities. When they showed up and scanned her Vial there was a number, just a code that they deciphered which meant they had to call Dr Malcolm himself, that he was the only one who could handle her death, being the daughter of his old partner. I just remember all these men in suits coming into the house and discussing things secretly. They were so formal and unconcerned with my feelings. Finally, right before they left, this one man reached out his hand to shake mine. He introduced himself as Doctor Paul Malcolm and said he was a friend of my grandfather and that if I ever needed anything, I should call him. He handed me his business card and quickly left. I remember he gave me the creeps; he was so poised and polished. I tucked the card inside one of those books that I'd gathered off the ground and never looked at it again. If I needed help, there was no way I was calling that man. That is, until now."

***

We continue driving for another hour, and as we near the city, the government buildings are visible on the horizon. The traffic has started to pick up and I can see flashing lights with cars pulled over to the side of the highway. Cars ahead are slowing down and starting to stop. I can't see far enough in front to work out what is going on, but it must be some kind of car accident or emergency. Then I hear sirens in the distance and three black sedans speed down the right-hand shoulder of the highway and stop up ahead. They all have Solution licence plates. Men in dark suits get out of the vehicles and walk over to cars stopped in line ahead of us. From where we are, it looks like they are starting to speak to people in the cars. After a few minutes, the line of cars starts to move, and one by one they get closer to our car.

I can see now several cars ahead that they have a briefcase pulled out with electrical equipment we've all come to recognise as a ParColm scanner.

"Shit, Milo, I think they're scanning people."

"Oh, fuck, you're right. I don't think I should be scanned, Dahl."

"But it should say you still have a couple of months left, right?"

"I mean, I think so, but who knows? I don't trust it at all. I have no idea what it will read."

Just then, three white Volvos pull up on the right side of the road and stop behind The Solution's sedans. Several men get out and come over and start talking to The Solution authorities. The car in front of us pulls ahead and drives off, and it's now our turn as the agent motions us to roll down our window.

"Afternoon, ma'am, sir." The man is wearing dark sunglasses. I can't see his eyes, but I tell by his chin tilt he's scanning the vehicle for occupants and notices the sleeping baby in the back. He hushes his voice. He must be a father.

"We've had a bit of an incident just down the road and we're scanning Vials just to clear the area. Will only take a second."

Before I have a chance to object, Milo starts talking. "Hey, man, our daughter just fell asleep back there. Any chance we can just keep going. It's been a tough ride."

"Sorry, sir, it's mandatory. I'm afraid I can't. Just following the rules."

As the agent reaches down towards his bag, I know exactly what he's about to pull out; but just then I notice the men from the white cars walking towards our vehicle. Immediately I recognise one of the men. "Kane!" I shout. My outburst instantly wakes up Violet, who starts screaming in the back seat.

My brother-in-law looks over in our direction and walks up to the car. "Dahlia. Hey! Fancy seeing you here. I thought I recognised this truck!" Kane walks over to the driver's side window and sees Milo sitting beside me. Shocked, he reaches his hand inside the truck. "Milo! Hey, man. Been a while." Kane looks over at me quizzically.

"Nice to see you, buddy." Milo shakes his hand, but quickly turns around, back to shushing Violet in the back seat. He places his hand on her lap and tries to rock her car seat to calm her.

"This guy bugging you?" Kane says loudly, trying to be heard above Violet's cries. He slaps the agent on the back and they shake hands. "Kane Montgomery. I should have known you guys would show up before too long." The agent scoffs mockingly at Kane.

"Just making sure you guys aren't crossing any lines. Heard about the incident; sounds like a doozy, but not sure disrupting innocent commuters is the right approach. This highway is going to get pretty backed-up before long. Think it's time you wrap this up."

"I hear you, Kane. You can take that up with my commanding officer over there." The agent motions to the group of men from both sides now passionately arguing about the situation.

"Will do. In the meantime, this is my sister-in-law, so can you let her on her way? She's got enough on her plate." Kane motions to Violet in the back seat and I catch his eye as he looks over at Milo. I know he's referring more to the mystery boyfriend that has suddenly reappeared than the crying baby.

"Uhhh, I guess. Sure, Kane. You're clear to go, ma'am." The man gives in. You can tell he's had these stand-offs with Kane in the past and doesn't have the energy to fight him on this one.

"Thank you," I say, not sure if I'm conveying how relieved I really am. "Thanks, Kane."

"Take care, you guys. Call your sister, Dahl. She's going to want to hear from you," Kane says with a wink as we drive off.

A couple of miles down the road, I let out a long exhale and feel for the first time the fear that must have plagued Milo for a lifetime. I take the next right into the city and pull over as I struggle to catch my breath. My chest is getting tight and I start to think I'm having a panic attack. "Oh my god, Milo! That was such a close call. Do you know what would have happened if they scanned you and it said you were past your Death Date?" I look over at Milo.

"Yes, I do, Dahlia. It's okay, just breathe. We're going to figure this out. Why don't you climb in the back with Violet and rest? I'll take over the driving."

I get out of the truck and walk around the front, meeting Milo in the middle. I grab onto him and pull him close. I bury myself into his body the way I always have and feel his strength envelop me. This is the first time we've really touched all day and feeling his body against mine is like coming home. He holds me for a long time until my breathing starts to calm down. He kisses me on the top of my head and brushes the hair off my face.

"Let's go find Dr Malcolm," he says.

***

I must have slept for at least an hour while Milo navigated the busy rush-hour streets of The Core. I wake up just as he's pulling into the parking lot of a motel.

"Hey, how are you feeling?" he says in a hushed voice.

I look over and see Violet is asleep beside me. She has her tiny fingers wrapped around my thumb. I sit up, careful not to wake her, and rub my shoulder that is sore from leaning against her hard car seat.

"I'm okay. Where are we?" I look around and see the neon flashing 'Vacancy' sign and a deserted outdoor pool to the side of the parking lot. There are rusty metal chairs piled up in the corner and an old water slide that looks like it could collapse at any moment.

"I thought we'd better get some rest for the night. Figure out our plan. This was the only place I could find in the city that had any vacancies. It's not a five-star, but it should be okay for the night, right? Unless you wanted to call Camellia. I know they are just a few blocks away…"

"No, this will be fine. I don't want to involve Camellia until I have answers for her millions of questions."

"That's what I figured. I'll go check us in."

As Milo walks away towards the office, I get out of the truck, quietly shutting the door behind me. I start to unload a few bags we'll need for the night from the back. I can see straight through to downtown of The Core from here, and The Solution's head office building literally scrapes the sky, dwarfing all the buildings around it. I can't help but wonder how we're going to just waltz in there and ask to speak to the creator of the place. I guess that's the plan we have to figure out tonight.

***

After we grab take-out from the greasy-spoon restaurant next door, Milo devours a club sandwich with extra avocado, now that he can finally eat it in front of me again, and we settle into the room for the night. I leave

Milo and Violet together while I grab a shower. It's hard to believe that it was just this morning when I last showered and was rehearsing what I was going to say to Mom at breakfast and Camden at lunch, telling them both that I was leaving. It feels like weeks have passed in this one day. Never could I have imagined I'd be reunited with Milo today and that he'd be back in our lives as if no time had passed. While I have been letting down my guard with him and witnessing his affection for Violet, I can't seem to let down the walls I have put up over the past couple of months for myself. With the bathroom door ajar, I can hear him talking so sweetly to Violet. "What a good girl you are. I'm sorry I haven't been here for you. I've missed you. You are so beautiful." These are the sounds I was expecting to hear every day, and they are heavenly. I'm hopeful that if I hear them enough, they will help heal the heaviness in my chest. After I've showered, I wipe the steam off the mirror and look down at the counter and notice I've missed two calls in the last half an hour. One is from Mom and one is from Camellia. I listen to the voicemails. Mom sounds calm but concerned as she just wants to check in and see if we made it to The Core okay. Camellia's, on the other hand, doesn't even start with hello — she just launches into twenty questions about Milo being back. Obviously, Kane filled her in and she has promised to keep calling every ten minutes if I don't call her back. What she lacks in emotion she makes up in perseverance. I call Mom back and am relieved to hear she is just on her way to see a movie with a couple of friends. Relieved because it already sounds like she's doing okay with me being gone, and relieved because then I don't have time to tell her about finding Milo! I can save that conversation for another day. I tell her I'll call again soon. Camellia, however, has nothing but time for questions.

"Okay, so tell me everything!" she says, answering after the first ring.

"Camellia, I'm in the bathroom of a motel room. I can't really get into it right now. Milo showed up just as I was leaving town."

"So, what, you just got in a car together and drove off into the sunset. Are you back together?" Her judgemental tone is very clear on the line.

"I don't know. I'm letting him spend time with Violet. And I'm helping him look into some stuff from his past."

"His past? What about his past? Where and what has he been doing this whole time? He may have wormed his way back in with you, but that's not going to work so easily on me."

"I know. I know. Just trust me, okay, Camellia? Everything is fine. I'll tell you more later. I have to go."

"Where are you? Did you go home? Is Mom okay?"

"We're in The Core, actually. We have to meet with someone tomorrow."

"You're in The Core? Why didn't you call me? Where are you staying? Does this have anything to do with your question about the database? Dahlia, what kind of stuff is Milo involved in?"

"Camellia! I can't right now. Please don't worry. I'll call you tomorrow, okay? I promise. Love you."

"Okay. I love you, too. Bye."

I'm shocked that Camellia is giving in and that she returned my affection.

"Bye." I hang up feeling guilty, but I need to see what happens with Dr Malcolm before I say anything more to Camellia. I can't afford to let anything slip about Milo. She needs to just keep thinking he was a deadbeat dad who ran out on his family, not the grandson of the creator of an establishment that she has spent her career fighting against. And especially not about his possibly faulty ParColm Vial. I don't even want to think about what she would do with that information. We need to get some answers first.

When I come out of the bathroom, I see Milo curled up in the bed on his side with his eyes closed and Violet tucked in beside him, fast asleep. I turn off the light and walk over to the bed, with just the bathroom light shining the way.

"I'm not asleep," Milo whispers, "but I think little princess here is."

I crouch down and pick up her little body and she lets out a deep sigh as I place her into her bassinet on the ground beside the bed.

"How's Camellia?" Milo asks. I can barely make out his face in the shadows, but I'm sure he is smirking.

"She's good. She has lots of questions, as you can imagine. I didn't tell her anything, don't worry, but I'll only be able to hold her off for so long. What's our plan then for tomorrow?"

"I think we just head to The Solution's building. I have my original birth certificate with my name as Milo Parisi. I'll ask to see Dr Malcolm and show his old business card you found in my book. Hopefully, that will work."

"Is there any chance they'll scan us?"

"I don't think so. There's no reason to do that in an office building. They only do that in medical situations, or if there has been some kind of event, right? But I don't know for sure. I'm wondering if my Vial has the same code built in that my Mom's did, that says that Dr Malcolm is to handle anything dealing with me, too. So that's one way we can get to him!"

"Oh, Milo, it's all so scary. What if we just go home? You have four months left. We can be a family, and then when that day comes, well… maybe you'll outlive that prognosis, too," I say, feeling myself getting emotional again.

"And then what? Hide for the rest of my life? I've been in hiding long enough. I need to know what's going on. I won't be any kind of father to Violet or partner to you if I don't get this figured out."

"Okay, I understand." I didn't really. But I thought of my Dad, who had fought against my Mom all those years ago to find out all of our fates. He couldn't live in limbo another day, and that decision led him to finding out his young son would soon die. As a mother now, that kind of pain is unimaginable, but Dad never did regret finding out. I have to be selfless and help Milo to find out the same thing about his future, or lack thereof.

***

Milo and I finally go to bed after midnight. It feels so strange to be in the room so close to him, but I'm still not ready to share a bed with him. I can't help but think this might be our last night together if things go as terribly as I fear they may tomorrow, but I am still so confused about how I feel about us. After I say goodnight, I can see the hurt in his eyes when I kiss him quickly and go towards the other double bed, alone. I turn myself towards the window and close my eyes, expecting to fall asleep quickly after the exhausting day we've had. But I can hear weird noises of the city outside the room and I can hear Milo breathing. I toss and turn for at least an hour until I can't handle it any more and I crawl in next to him. His bed is so warm and his body is so familiar, I slide myself in close next to him and he lets out a deep sigh as he wakes. "Hi," he whispers, "took you long enough."

Our mouths find each other and we kiss like we're strangers again, slow and softly at first until our muscle memory takes over and it's like no time has been lost at all. We start removing clothing under the covers, when suddenly a cry comes out of Violet's bassinet.

"Did we wake her?" Milo asks.

"I don't think so. That's not her usual cry." I throw on Milo's t-shirt and rush over to her. I scoop her up and feel instantly that she is extremely warm.

"I think she has a fever. In my bag in the bathroom there is Baby Tylenol. Can you grab it?" I unwrap her from her sleeping swaddle and hold her close to my chest, trying to rock her close to calm her down. Milo comes back with the medicine and after I give her some and find her soother, I lean back against the headboard of the bed and hum a quiet lullaby. "It's okay, sweetie, you'll feel better soon." Milo lays down beside us and that's how the three of us spend the rest of the night. We each take shifts rocking Violet while she bobs in and out of sleep until the sun starts peeking through the paper-thin drapes of the motel room window.

***

"I don't want to take her with us today, Milo. She's so exhausted from last night," I say, yawning, as we are packing up in the motel room.

"Of course. Do you want to stay here while I go?"

"No! I want to come with you. I'm going to call Camellia and see if we can drop her off at their house. We have no idea what is going to happen when we get there, and I don't want to take a feverish baby with us."

After another quick phone call to Camellia, when she bombards me with more questions and I remain aloof, we find ourselves at her front door.

"Come in, come in. Hi, Milo. Nice to see you," Camellia says in her most diplomatic voice. "How is she?"

"She's much better. Her fever has gone down and her appetite seems back, so I've left you lots of bottles of milk in her bag. I'm sure she'll just sleep for you mostly, but if there are any issues just call."

"Of course. I cancelled all my meetings this morning, so we are just going to cuddle on the couch, aren't we, sweetie?" Camellia takes Violet from my arms and rests her comfortably against her shoulder. "Don't worry about us."

"Thank you, Camellia. We owe you," Milo says.

"The Auntie babysitting is free, but you two owe me some serious answers when you get back!" Camellia says, as she closes the door behind us.

As we get back into the truck, I feel the weight of a thousand pounds push down on my heart as we drive away from my sick baby; but maybe it's more likely the gravity of where we are headed and what we will find out.

Chapter Twenty-Four
Dahlia — DD in 54 years, 7 months, 7 days

The Solution's headquarters spans several city blocks of dark heavy marble and glass rising up from the ground in intricate hexagon patterns. The building is a cold pale grey colour from the outside, but once we walk into the lobby it is a stark white space that feels bare and sterile. There is a long desk with one woman behind glass. I look around and notice there are no chairs or plants or anything to make the lobby comfortable, or even inviting. "I guess they don't want people loitering in here," I say under my breath, as we approach the woman behind the glass.

We walk over to the desk and wait uncomfortably for the woman to address us. Instead, she just looks up from her computer screen but doesn't say a word, as if our mere presence is a waste of her time.

"Uh… hello there. We'd like to speak to Dr Paul Malcolm." Milo coughs as he says the name. It does seem almost unbelievable hearing it said out loud.

"Excuse me. Did you say Dr Malcolm?" The lady behind the glass is now standing and moving away from her computer. I notice her hand is reaching behind her back, feeling for something under the desk. I realise she must be signalling a silent alarm of some kind.

"Yes, that's right. I have his card here. He knows who I am." Milo also seems to have noticed the heightened awareness from the lady, who is now looking past us towards a hallway just out of view.

"Okay. Please, just wait one moment while security comes to assist you." The woman looks relieved as three men in black suits come quickly down the hallway towards us.

Milo starts reaching inside his jacket for the business card when the men yell for him to stand still. "Sorry. I was just reaching for the business card."

"We just need to scan you, sir," says the biggest of the three men, as he stands a foot taller than Milo and peers down on us.

"Uhh, no thank you. I'd rather not have my ParColm Vial scanned. I just need to talk to Dr Malcolm."

I look over at the two men, trying to hide my fear. We've been in this building for less than two minutes and they are already trying to scan Milo. I frantically try and think of some distraction, some way for us to just leave now.

"We understand that, sir, but we can't just let anyone in to meet Dr Malcolm. For security reasons, we have to follow a strict protocol. A quick scan and then we'll be able to find out what business you have with Dr Malcolm." The man reaches down into his pocket and pulls out a phone-sized black apparatus. "Just a body scan, that is. For metal, weapons, explosives, that kind of thing."

"Oh. Right. Yes, no problem, man." Milo gives me a relieved sideways glance and they run the object up and down Milo's body.

"You too, ma'am."

After they are done, they take us back to the desk, where the lady is back to being distracted by her computer. "They're clear. You can find out what business they have here today." The three men walk away back down the hallway without another word to us.

"Right. So you said, Dr Malcolm, but he's not expecting you. Is that right? He doesn't really take unsolicited visitors." The receptionist continues to give us the very minimum of her attention as she types away at her computer.

"I bet. Look, it's very important that we speak to him. Maybe if I showed you some ID that would help move this along?" Milo reaches down into his pocket and pulls out his birth certificate. He opens up the folded document and puts it down on the desk top.

"I don't really know what good this will do…" The receptionist pauses as she glances down and reads the name out loud, slowly and dramatically: "M-I-L-O-P-A-R-I-S-I… Parisi. Oh! Yes, I see. Sorry for the delay. Please head down the hallway to the left. Someone will meet you on the other side," she says, as she picks up the phone next to her while staring at Milo. As we start to walk towards the hallway, I look back at the receptionist, who is now speaking to someone on the phone. "Prepare the boardroom. Doctor M has visitors. Parisi. Yes, that's the name. Exactly. Thank you."

Milo and I make our way slowly down a crisp white hallway with dim overhead lighting. There are elevator doors lining both sides, with no clear place to wait.

"I can't believe all it took was my last name for us to get a meeting so quickly," Milo whispers, as we stand awkwardly, waiting.

"I know! I think it's a good sign that this is going to go well." I give Milo's damp hand a reassuring squeeze. I'm so relieved we'll be able to see Dr Malcolm so quickly and that we didn't have to explain anything further to anyone else. Although maybe I'm being naive thinking that the co-inventor of the ParColm Vial will be a friend and not a foe. After all, he is the other half of the 'Doctor Evil' duo whose sole purpose was to end lives, not help extend them. Before I have a chance to dwell on all the terrible things that could happen, an elevator dings and opens up to reveal a middle-aged woman in a grey suit and holding a black briefcase. "Mr Parisi. Please come with me." Milo and I give each other a discreet look as we walk into the elevator with the woman and the door closes. She presses floor 63 and we ride in awkward silence as the floors pass by one after another. When the doors open on floor 63, the lady in the suit extends an arm, gesturing for us to get out. "Please make yourselves comfortable. Someone will be with you shortly." The doors to the elevator close and she disappears behind them.

Floor 63 is as sparse and sterile as the rest of the building, but from this height the view out of the wrap-around glass windows is extraordinary. I can't help but walk right up to the glass to try to orient myself to the landmarks outside. I find the river and follow that towards the edge of The Core, and behind a couple of buildings I can just make out the condo complex where Camellia and Kane live. Milo must be thinking the same thing and tells me to give Camellia a call if I want, to check on Violet. "No, it's okay. She would call if there were any problems. Let's just wait."

We both take a seat on a large white leather sofa, holding hands and jointly holding our breaths. We wait like this for ten minutes before some glass doors open to the side and in walks a short, balding man who looks to be in his sixties.

"Mr Parisi, good morning. Please follow me." Without shaking hands, the man starts leading us into a large glass room with a big metal conference table with dozens of chairs all around it.

"Is this Dr Malcolm?" I say under my breath. "He seems pretty young."

"No, I don't think so. It can't be," Milo says.

"Please have a seat, Mr. Parisi and …" He puts out his hand and I go in to shake it, but instead he drops a leather briefcase on the table and starts removing papers.

"Miss Dobbs," I say quietly, as I look down at the briefcase. I see it's engraved.

Mitchell MacLeod

Attorney

Stevens MacLeod & Murphy, Law firm

"Very well. Mr Parisi, Miss Dobbs. Since you didn't give any notice of your visit today, I don't have a lot of time in my schedule for this meeting, so I will get straight to it. Mr Parisi, my firm has represented Dr Malcolm and your grandfather Dr Parisi since they first began their project with the ParColm Vial decades ago. As that expanded into what we now recognise as The Solution, I'm sure you can imagine what an important account this entire corporation and its founder is to our firm. Now, I'm not sure what was communicated to you by your mother, but I can assure you that my client has an iron-clad case that your inheritance from your grandfather is more than generous and continues to offer a very comfortable endowment. Now, I have been informed that the legacy department of The Solution, also known as The Resolution, has been trying to contact you for some time to work out the details now that there is a next of kin. Is that correct?"

Milo and I look at each other in disbelief. Resolution handles inheritance. The paperwork filed at the hospital after Violet was born must have connected up with Milo's files, and she's entitled to money from

The Solution. I can see in Milo's eyes his relief that whoever was following him wasn't a threat after all. But his relief shortly turns to anger as he slams down his fist on the table.

"Mr MacLeod, I am not here today to discuss money!" Milo rises from his chair and walks over to within an inch of Mitchell Macleod's face. "I NEED TO TALK TO DOCTOR MALCOLM!" Milo slams down Dr Malcolm's card hard onto the table it flips over to the backside, revealing the small embossed symbols of the two triangles and the stars with initials AP<**>PM.

Mitchell MacLeod looks down at the card and immediately pushes himself back from the table and stands up. Something about seeing that symbol has changed his demeanour entirely. "I'm sorry. I didn't realise you had one of those cards. This does change things. Please excuse me for a moment." Mitchell MacLeod stumbles on his way to the glass door, sliding it open just enough to squeeze out and closing it roughly behind him.

"Can you believe this? Money! Mon…" Milo starts pacing the room angrily.

"Shhh! I can hear him out there. Listen." I press myself up against the wall and strain to hear what is going on in the hallway. I can just make out Mitchell MacLeod on the phone, yelling in a hushed voice at someone on the other end.

"Olivia, find out where Malcolm is. Yes, I know he's not in, he's never in, he's a senile old man, but that doesn't change the fact that Parisi's grandson has one of the cards. The ones with the symbols. Exactly. I know. Yes, I've never actually seen one of these in person either. Trust me, I have other things I need to be doing, too, but you know the instructions: if one of these is presented it is a direct link to Malcolm. He must be contacted immediately. So, get him here now!"

I rush back to my seat and motion for Milo to do the same, just as Mitchell MacLeod comes back in the room.

"Sorry about that. We're working on getting Dr Malcolm available for you. I'm afraid he's not in the building today. He doesn't spend much time here any more, but that little piece of cardstock you have is very persuasive and has a way of making him appear out of thin air." Mitchell MacLeod looks down at the card again and makes a motion like he's losing his tie. "I'll have someone bring in some coffee and refreshments while you wait. Again, apologies for earlier. I'm sure you can understand there have been a lot of people over the years who have tried to get money out of this corporation, and especially its founders. We have to treat everyone as a potential threat these days."

"Sure. We get it. No worries." Milo sits down next to me and lets out a deep exhale.

"You'll have to excuse me now. I have another appointment I'm late for." Just as Mitchell MacLeod gets up to leave, the same short woman with the blunt brown haircut in the grey suit comes into the room.

"This is Dr Olivia Evans, Dr Malcolm's assistant. She will take care of you until he arrives. You two take care."

"Hello. Dr Malcolm is on his way in. It shouldn't be too long. He's asked me to bring you to his private floor. It will be more comfortable for you. Please follow me."

Milo and I get up and follow Dr Evans back out to the hallway of elevators and into one with its doors already open. Dr Evans swipes a card and presses the M at the top of all of the numbers. We go up another dozen floors and the elevator opens up to a completely different world from the rest of what we'd seen of this building. It is a cluttered room with dark, oversized wood furniture. There is a big mahogany desk at the far end of the room with a giant grey landscape painting above, and below the desk is scattered with papers and small pieces of electronics. There are two big brown leather couches that look very worn and old. The glass windows of The Solution's headquarters blast light from all angles into the entire building, but in here the light is entirely blocked out by thick ceiling-to-floor velvet drapes. In front of us is an ornate square wooden table with chairs all around it. It looks like an antique dining room table that belongs in an old English manor house and not the penthouse of a building that revolutionised social sciences and the re-engineering of an entire population.

Before either of us have a chance to comment on the decor, Dr Evans motions to the table, where there has been coffee, fruit and pastries left out. "Please make yourselves comfortable. The wait shouldn't be too much longer."

Milo moves towards the coffee pot and as he reaches for a cup, he turns his body towards the grand desk for the first time and gasps loudly. "That's one of my paintings! It was sold at an auction years ago to an anonymous bidder. I never did find out where it ended up. That is so bizarre."

"Dr Malcolm collects quite a bit of art. He keeps most of it at home, but insisted this one be hung in his office. You'll have to ask him about it when he gets here," Dr Evans says with a smirk on her face. She obviously has no poker face and knows more about the painting and its significance than she is letting on. "Now, if you're all set up here, I'll leave you. Be well." She lets herself out of the door and it closes quietly behind her.

Milo has now moved himself right up against his painting behind Dr Malcolm's desk chair. "This is so creepy, isn't it? Why would he have one of my paintings? It can't be a coincidence. I remember the person who bought it completely overbid and paid a small fortune for this one. It was my first really big sale. I bought my first car with the money."

"Do you think Dr Malcolm has been keeping tabs on you all these years?" I ask. "It would make sense, since you're the only living relative of his dead partner."

"I mean, I guess so. But why? It's not like I ever knew my grandfather. He died before I was born. My mom had been estranged from him for years before he died."

"He was a great man and he loved your mother a great deal." Milo and I both whip our heads around at the sound of the voice coming from the doorway at the far end of the room. "Private elevator. Sorry to startle you. Paul Malcolm. Dahlia, is it? Pleasure to meet you."

I instinctively walk over to the outstretched hand of this handsome, statuesque man. Even at his age, which must be in the late seventies, he commands a presence. He has a full very neatly trimmed grey and black beard and wide-rimmed black glasses. He is wearing a white lab coat that looks as though it has been ironed with its perfect creases down the sides. He has on a light blue striped dress shirt and a navy tie that matches the deep blue of his eyes. It takes me a second to realise I haven't said anything back and have just been staring. "Er, hello. Thank you for coming to see us so quickly," I sputter out.

"And Milo. Good to see you again, son." Dr Malcolm walks over to the desk where Milo is still standing. "It's a beautiful piece. I find it very calming." Dr Malcolm motions up at the painting above. "What was your inspiration?"

"Loss. Despair. Loneliness. The usual stuff," Milo says coldly, and he joins me back over by the table.

"I see. That's why I love art so much. It's so subjective. Unlike science."

"Why do you have it?" Milo asks bluntly.

"That's a good question. I'm a collector of all sorts of things: antique cars, French wine; but my art collection brings me the most pleasure." Dr Malcolm pauses for a moment with a thin smile on his lips. "But you want to know why I have one of *your* paintings. Do you find it creepy? Is that the word you used? I have to admit it is not a coincidence. Whether you have known it or not, I consider you a part of my family, Milo. Your grandfather meant a great deal to me, and with your mother having passed on, I wanted to make sure you were okay. And then you turned into a famous painter and I just couldn't resist purchasing one of your pieces. Lucky me!"

"Sorry, back up. You've been checking up on me?" Milo asks.

"I've respected your mother's wishes and kept a distance, but yes. I made a promise to your grandfather to keep an eye out for your mother." Dr Malcolm pauses for a while. He removes his glasses and cleans them on his tie. "I failed in that regard, I'm afraid. All the more reason to make things right for you. And from my observations, things are going very well for you. No?" Dr Malcolm smiles warmly in my direction. "Or at least they were. And then you showed up here today and presented one of those cards. Now that can't be a good sign."

"What is it with the cards?" I blurt out. "It got us taken care of pretty quickly."

"Yes, that is what they were designed for. Dr Parisi and I were under a lot of demand, especially in the beginning. When the ParColm Vials were first launched, we had people coming out of the woodwork from everywhere with demands and threats, and it took our time and attention away from our work, which was paramount. We each had a handful of those cards made up with our own special symbol and they were distributed to the people who really needed immediate access to us. It's a direct link to us, so that no matter what we were working on, we could be interrupted. Now that The Solution has become the mega-corporation it has, everything is handled through their various departments. I had forgotten there were any of these left in circulation."

"You gave me one the day my mother died," Milo says, with his eyes downcast.

"Yes, I did. I remembered that when they said it was you who had presented it today. I honestly expected you to use it earlier, for help with college tuition or buying a house. Maybe some art connections. I don't know. You really are family, Milo. You could have reached out."

"Your lawyer Mitchell MacLeod doesn't share the same views," I say sarcastically.

"No, I guess he wouldn't. But he's looking out for the corporation. He doesn't care about the sacrifices Dr Parisi and I made. The toll this entire thing had on our families. The toll this took on your life. Your mother's. But I do."

"My mother always trusted you. She didn't speak about my grandfather at all, but at the end of her life… when she wasn't at her most lucid" — Milo paused — "she said if I ever needed help that I should find you. That's why we're here today. I hope she's right that I can trust you."

"You can, Milo. I promise you that. I wish I could have done more for your mother. Believe me, I tried. We don't need to get into that now. Please tell me what I can do for you."

Milo takes a deep breath and glances my way. I nod at him my reassurance from across the room. "It's my Vial. Something is wrong with it," he says.

"What do you mean, *wrong*?"

I can't help myself and I blurt out, "Well, he was supposed to die when he was seven and didn't, and now it says he's going to die in six months and we just want to know if he is."

"You had it scanned? Didn't your mother tell you not to do that?" Dr Malcolm gets up from his chair and walks over to his desk. He opens up a drawer and pulls out a ParColm scanner.

"She did, yes. But… there was a medical situation and… I had it scanned. It was an emergency." Milo looks over at me and I am confused why he doesn't mention our daughter, but realise he must want to keep some parts of his life a secret from Dr Malcolm, although I wonder if that's even possible. It seems this man knows everything.

Dr Malcolm places the scanner on the table in front of us. We all stare at it for several seconds, before I can't stand the tension any more. "Well, aren't you going to scan him?" I realise I'm shouting.

"No. I'm not. Milo, you're not going to die in six months. Or six years. Or sixty years. At least, I don't think so."

"You don't THINK so! Isn't that the entire point of this whole bullshit contraption? That there is no more thinking. You two took that out of the equation entirely!" I point at a picture hanging on the wall from a newspaper clipping when Dr Malcolm looked thirty years younger, with long black wavy hair, standing next to the statuesque Dr Parisi, with a long salt and pepper beard and dishevelled suit. The two men are holding a prototype of a ParColm Vial, both with knowing smiles like they understand they are about to change the future.

"Yes, you're right. That was the point. And we saved humanity, didn't we? At a cost. We've all lost people, Miss Dobbs. I know about your father and I'm sorry. That was very recently and I understand your feelings must be very raw. And you're worried you're going to lose your boyfriend soon, too. Well, I can assure you that won't happen." Dr Malcolm takes a seat behind his desk and removes his glasses. He takes out a bottle of a dark liquor from one of the cabinets behind him and begins to pour three glasses.

"We don't need a drink!" Milo says in an impatient tone.

"I disagree. I don't tell this story very often, and when I do, I find it easier with a glass in my hand." Dr Malcolm ignores Milo's wishes and motions for us to both come grab our glass. Like obedient children, we do. "When I met Ignacio Parisi, I was a grad student working on one of his many studies. We worked for years together before he finally trusted me to be a part of the development of his vial. By then he had become like a father to me and taught me more about life and science than anyone I had ever known. He was a brilliant man, but a complicated one. He adored the fame and notoriety we received, but was reluctant to be in the spotlight. He shouldered all the backlash of the Dr Evil bullshit and never let it get to him. Even after all the protesting and rioting, he was resolute in his beliefs that we were doing good. That our 'solution' was the right one. It cost him everything. He would spend days and nights at the lab. This really was his only love, and everything else came second. His marriage, his daughter, his sanity. So, when it came time for us to each draw a random vial ourselves, to prove once and for all we wholeheartedly believed in The Solution, I chose the vial with the two weeks left to live and Parisi chose fifty-two years."

"But Dr Parisi was the one who died right after," I said.

"Yes, he did. He traded with me. I had a young family and a life beyond The Solution. Parisi was not the monster everyone made him out to be. He cared for me. He made the ultimate sacrifice in dying for what he believed in, and look at what a difference he made in this world. He's a hero. After he died, I promised myself I would watch out for his family. He gave me the gift of life, so I vowed to do what I could to give that to the people he had loved." Dr Malcolm rises from his chair and finishes his drink, tipping his head back to get every ounce down.

"You have an empty Vial, Milo. To repay my mentor for his selflessness, I have spared his grandson from our salvation. I oversaw everything myself so there would be no trail, because even *I* can't save you if this ever gets discovered. You were given a fake death certificate, and thankfully your mother was scared enough to never report it. I had your Vial set up to give off a random reading if ever scanned, hence the six months, but you will die of natural causes tomorrow or in ninety years, Milo. As the descendant of this entire dynasty, ironically you get an exception." Dr Malcolm chuckles silently, clearly very proud of himself.

Both Milo and I sit in stunned silence for several minutes. Dr Malcolm reaches over to pour himself another glass, as Milo and I sit with the juggernaut of information that Milo has no set expiry date like the rest of us. He will just die when he dies. This concept is so foreign and unfathomable.

"I tried to help your mother in the same way…" — the bravado in Dr Malcolm's voice starts to waiver — "but it wasn't so successful, I'm afraid."

"What do you mean?" Milo demands.

"It was shortly after your grandfather died. I was a mess, dealing with the loss of my hero and how I would shoulder the burden of this entire corporation alone. I made a rash decision and it had very negative consequences." Dr Malcolm turns his body away from us as he pours himself another drink and takes a long, slow sip. "Your mother had been in a car crash coming home from a college football game. I was alerted that she was in the hospital for minor injuries and would be spending the night just for observation. I decided this was my chance to repay your grandfather for his sacrifice in saving my life. I would save your mother's. Do the same thing I did for you — switch out her ParColm Vial for a fake one. Only the surgery did not go as planned. There were complications and, well, from what I understand, it led her down a path of horrible pain that resulted in her substance abuse. I tried to give her life; instead, I believe I took it from her that day. I'll never forgive myself."

"That's why she had those headaches? She was in pain because of you!" Milo says, as he wipes away tears that have started to fill up his eyes. "I always thought it was my fault somehow. I always blamed myself. But it was you. It was because of you, you fucking asshole. When was she supposed to die? Would she still be here today?" Milo shouts across the room at a now shrunken Dr Malcolm.

"I'm afraid so, Milo. But I'm sure deep down you know you were the happiness in her life. You kept her going all those years, even though her pain was slowly killing her."

We all sit in silence for several minutes as the information starts to settle in around us. The room feels mustier than ever now that these big secrets have been unearthed. After a while, I finally get up the courage to speak, as both men look up at me.

"Sorry to state the obvious here, but what happens if someone finds out that Milo doesn't have a real Vial?"

"Exactly what you think. They'll kill you. It's only fair. So, don't get caught. You've managed to evade the authorities this long. Keep it up, kid. Your grandfather would be proud." And just like, that Dr Malcolm's self-assuredness kicks back in.

"What if I don't want this? Can't you change it out? Give me a new one. I'll take my chances with whatever date it says. I've been living in fear for most of my life, and especially these past few weeks. I don't want this. I don't want this for my family." Milo turns to me with tears in his eyes. He's so caught up with emotion, he lets the word 'family' slip, although it's pretty safe to assume that if Dr Malcolm knew about my dad dying, he probably knows about Violet as well.

"No can do, I'm afraid. I can't tamper with it now. I don't have the access to things I used to. I lean on Dr Evans to help me out here and there with bigger challenges, but I'm just a glorified poster boy at this point. They put me up here on the top floor, away from the real work. They gave me access to one of the old labs with a small staff and we tinker around a bit, but I couldn't change things for you now, even if I wanted to. And I don't. Consider yourself lucky, my boy!" Dr Malcolm says. "Now I realise this is a lot of information to take in all at once, but I'm afraid I have a prior engagement. It was so nice to see you both and I hope you will keep in touch. I'll be keeping an eye out for your paintings. You'll probably have a lot of material to work with now." Dr Malcolm smiles unapologetically as he walks backwards towards the elevator. "Go home. Enjoy your life. Take care of that little girl of yours and be a better father than your grandfather was."

***

Milo and I walk out into the fresh air of the street in a daze. We make our way in silence towards the truck parked a couple of blocks away. After so much silence, I finally ask Milo how he is.

"I don't know, Dahlia. It's a lot. I know I should be happy; I have a sort of gift I guess that some people would kill for, but it's also such a shock I can't even begin to process it."

"I know. I think it will help to talk about it, though — when you're ready. I'm here for you."

"You're worried I'm going to go AWOL again like I did after my Mom died, aren't you?"

"I guess, maybe! I don't know. Or you'll just disappear like you just did the last time you got some troubling news. I don't know what you're going to do, but I'm scared to death."

"Scared to death. What a choice of words!" Milo mutters under his breath. "Listen, Dahlia, I can't promise you I'm not going to be a little messed up after this, but I'm not going anywhere. I lived apart from you and Violet for two months and it nearly broke me, so there's no way I'm going to do that again. All I know is that when I woke up this morning, I thought I only had a few months left with you two; and now... well, now I get to watch our daughter grow up. So, I just want to go home. I want to be a family; I want to see Maria and Miguel for the time we have left with them and I want to paint. I'm going to need to take this day by day, but if you'll have me, I promise to make up the time we lost and be there for you and Violet for as long as I have left on this earth. What do you say?"

"I say — what are we going to tell Camellia?" I smile at Milo and pull him into me. We lean up against Dad's rusty red truck and kiss in the sunshine. Suddenly, my thoughts turn to my Dad, and I picture him somewhere surrounded by crystal blue water at the stern of a canoe, with Rowan up at the bow. I have no idea what is going to happen for Milo and me now, but I'm hopeful for our future. There have been a lot of moments of pain over the past few months, but just as many joyful ones, and this one now is a happy moment... and I plan to hang on to it for as long as I can.

Epilogue
Dahlia — DD in 53 years, 9 months, 9 days

Around Violet's first birthday, we finally complete the renovations on our home. Milo is unpacking boxes into Violet's bedroom, with its bright yellow walls and farm animal mural he painted for her. "Moo-cow. Neyyyyy. Hor-seee" are the sweet sounds I can hear coming from her bedroom.

When we returned back to my house after our ordeal in The Core, we were reunited with Maria and Miguel, who had just returned from their big overseas trip. They were overjoyed to see Violet and surprised and relieved to see Milo. We never did discuss his lost time, although I have a feeling Miguel may have let Maria in on Milo's secret visit after all. Everyone was just so happy to be together and cherish our few months left with them.

One night after one of Maria's feasts, they handed us a manilla envelope. "It's the deed to our house. We want you to have it when we pass; and with the few months we have left, we are going to help you renovate it into one big home for the three of you. There will be space for Violet to have a proper little girl's bedroom, and an office for you, Dahlia," Maria said.

Then Miguel pipped in, "And you can turn my workshop into your studio, Milo."

"That's right! It's time for you to get rid of that silly old loft and be here. Properly." These were Maria's orders, and, of course, no other answer would have been accepted by them from us — except yes! And thank you! And tears. Many, many happy and bittersweet tears. And the tears continued to fall just like the leaves on the ground as we said goodbye to our dear sweet friends on a crisp October day. Their lives were celebrated with a full catholic mass attended by so many loved ones: people were spilling out the door. It was no surprise their love and generosity were felt by so many, but none were more grateful than our little family for everything they had done for us, from first bringing us together to caring for us when we needed it most, to finally making our house a home.

***

"Hey, hun, come here for a second," Milo shouts down the hall at me.

I save what I've been working on on my computer in my newly-decorated home office and make my way down the hallway lined with black-and-white pictures of Violet from the past year. I come into the room and see Milo is holding up my hospital bag. He must have found it buried under all the boxes in Violet's closet.

Milo reaches in and starts pulling out all the items he'd packed up a year ago: blankets, baby onesies, soothers. "That's where that thing ended up. I forgot all about it. I threw that bag in here last year once we got home from the hospital. I never could bring myself to unpack it. It just reminded me too much of you; and those first weeks and months after she was born it was too hard for me to go there. I was just in survival mode," I say.

Milo pulls me in and with his arm around my shoulders, gives Violet a kiss on the forehead. "I'm so sorry. If I could do it all again…" He trails off.

"I know." I kiss him softly on the lips. There is no need to hash up the 'lost months'.

"Hey, here's that book I've been looking for. I've been reading Violet the one my Mom gave me all this time. I wondered where the copy was that I'd bought."

Milo opens up the book and I read over his shoulder the inscription I had seared into my brain last year:

To my girls.

When you read this book, think of me and know that I am with you both always. Trust in me. This is not the end and I will make this right.

Violet grabs the book from Milo and turns it upside down, flipping through the pages. "Vivi's book," Violet says, as she backs herself up and plops down on Milo's lap, ready to be read a story. Milo tries unsuccessfully to get the book out of Violet's hands to read to her, as she bends the spine back too far.

"Violet, careful with the book. You have to be gentle. Gentle," he says slowly, while rubbing the book, demonstrating to our feisty one-year-old.

Violet grabs the book back and throws it over her head hard onto the ground, while she lets out an adorable little giggle and says, "ENTLE".

"No, that's not gentle." Milo kisses her on top of the head. As he bends over to pick up the book, a small piece of paper falls out. A business card folded in half. Shivers run up my entire body as I see the familiar scalloped edges of the card stock and the AP<**>PM symbol on the back. I shoot a glance at Milo, who is having the same reaction as me. Violet goes to reach for the card, just as Milo swipes it up from the ground.

"Mine!" she yells, and starts to cry.

I grab Violet in my arms and stroke her hair, hushing to soothe her. Milo unfolds the card and flips it over to show me. There is no need. I know what name it will say. Dr Paul Malcolm.

"This bag hasn't been opened since the day Violet and I left the hospital. Was Dr Malcolm there? Does that mean…?"

Milo cuts me off. "Violet doesn't have a Death Date either!"

THE END

9 781784 659905